FROM THE
NANCY DREW FILES

THE CASE: Nancy tries to track down the slippery saboteur who has turned a dreamworld into a living nightmare.

CONTACT: Supermodel Martika Sawyer is desperate: her entire future rides on Cloud Nine.

SUSPECTS: Christina Adams — *The health spa queen and Martika's rival, she'd like nothing better than to see Cloud Nine go up in smoke.*

Kurt Yeager — *World-famous athlete and Martika's former fiancé, he seethes with resentment over the breakup of their engagement.*

Derek Sawyer — *Martika's brother, he's a notorious gambler who's deep in debt; now his sister has threatened to cut him off.*

COMPLICATIONS: The beautiful Martika is a woman of many talents — one of which is making enemies. But for Nancy the trick is getting at the truth . . . on an island of illusion, disguise, and deceit.

Books in The Nancy Drew Files® Series

Available from ARCHWAY Paperbacks

The Nancy Drew Files™

Case 91
If Looks Could Kill
Carolyn Keene

AN ARCHWAY PAPERBACK
Published by POCKET BOOKS
New York   London   Toronto   Sydney   Tokyo   Singapore

AN ARCHWAY PAPERBACK *Original*

An Archway Paperback published by
POCKET BOOKS, a division of Simon & Schuster Inc.
1230 Avenue of the Americas, New York, NY 10020

Copyright © 1994 by Simon & Schuster Inc.
Produced by Mega-Books of New York, Inc.

ISBN: 0-671-79483-3

First Archway Paperback printing January 1994

10 9 8 7 6 5 4 3 2 1

NANCY DREW, AN ARCHWAY PAPERBACK and colophon are registered trademarks of Simon & Schuster Inc.

THE NANCY DREW FILES is a trademark of Simon & Schuster Inc.

Cover art by Tricia Zimic

Printed in the U.S.A.

IL 6+

If Looks Could Kill

Chapter

One

"Nancy, TELL ME this isn't the life!"

Nancy Drew shaded her eyes with her hand and glanced over at her friend Bess Marvin, who was lying on the lounge chair next to hers.

"It's fantastic," Nancy agreed, brushing her reddish blond hair back. "Right, George?" Nancy asked.

Bess's cousin, George Fayne, sighed contentedly from the lounge chair on the other side of Nancy. "Heaven," she replied.

The three girls were on board a luxurious yacht owned by supermodel Martika Sawyer, heading out of the harbor of Charlotte Amalie, on the island of St. Thomas, in the U.S. Virgin Islands. From their spot near the stern, they watched the town's lovely whitewashed buildings grow smaller and smaller as the boat neared the headland

1

on the west side of the harbor. In less than an hour they would dock at Rainbow Cay, where they'd be spending the week as Martika's guests for the grand opening of her resort spa, Cloud Nine.

"I still can't believe it," Bess went on. "A week at a brand-new resort spa on a private island in the middle of the Caribbean, getting in shape, eating healthy food—"

"Easy on the food, Bess," George interrupted, "even if it *is* healthy. You said you wanted to lose weight this week."

"Don't be a killjoy, George," Bess said. "Remember, this vacation is free, thanks to Nancy."

Nancy lay back, closed her eyes, and contemplated how it had all come about. Her father, the lawyer Carson Drew, had once done some work for the world-famous model and had told Martika about his daughter's detective work. Then, five days earlier, Nancy had gotten a call from Martika.

"I have a problem that I don't want to talk about over the phone," Martika had said. "Could you please come to the opening of my new resort? As my guest, of course. You see, I'm afraid there may be some trouble."

Nancy had wanted to ask questions, but Martika had been firm about not answering any of them until Nancy came down to Cloud Nine. "Bring a friend or two," Martika had said.

"You'll have a wonderful time, and you'll be doing me an enormous favor."

Nancy was convinced—the chance to bring George and Bess had been irresistible. A week in the Caribbean with her two best friends, and a mystery to solve. The perfect vacation!

Nancy opened her eyes and realized that the yacht was now out of the harbor. It was hugging the southwest coast of St. Thomas, which was dotted with colorful villas and hotels. She glanced toward the bow, where a group of people were gathered. They appeared to be Martika Sawyer's celebrity guests. She had invited them to join the paying customers for the opening of Cloud Nine.

"George," she said, focusing on one of them. "The guy in the Cloud Nine polo shirt. Isn't that Kurt Yeager?"

George took off her mirrored sunglasses to get a better look. "It is!" she said excitedly. "Wow!"

"Who's he?" Bess wanted to know.

"The former world decathlon champion, that's who," George replied.

"He *does* look familiar, now that you mention it," Bess said. "And gorgeous, too. Was he in any movies?"

"As a matter of fact, he did do some acting after he retired from competition," George said.

"Wasn't he in *The Flame Throwers?*" Nancy asked.

3

"Yes. Unfortunately it was one of the biggest flops of the past five years," George said. "I guess being in it kind of finished his movie career."

"Now I remember where I saw him!" Bess said suddenly. "He was in *Celeb* magazine. He used to be engaged to Martika Sawyer!"

"That's right," George said. "Well, I guess they must still be good friends if Martika invited him to the opening of her spa."

"If I remember right, they just broke up last winter," Bess said. "It was kind of rough."

Nancy watched Kurt closely. He had a clipboard in his hands, and he seemed to be making checks on a list of some kind. Was Kurt Yeager a guest or was he working for Martika Sawyer?

At that moment Kurt detached himself from the little group and wandered back to Nancy and her friends, his California-blond hair gleaming in the sun. "Hi," he said, smiling down at the three of them. "I'm Kurt Yeager."

"Yes, we know," Bess told him, giving him a big smile. "I'm Bess, and this is Nancy, and this is George. She's an athlete, too."

George rolled her eyes at her cousin, then turned to Kurt. "I'm a big fan of yours. I watched you win the world championships the last time you competed. You were incredible."

"Thanks," Kurt said. "Yeah, those were the good old days. Now I'm in a different business—director of guest services and fitness supervisor for Cloud Nine." He smiled and heaved a little sigh. "Well, if you'll tell me your last names, I'll check you off my list."

So he *is* working for Martika, Nancy thought to herself as George told Kurt their last names. Kurt and Martika must have patched things up if he was on her staff at Cloud Nine.

"I do sports training sessions and exercise classes," he told them. "I hope you sign up for some of them so we can get to know one another. In fact, I'm giving a body-sculpting demonstration later today. Why don't you come?" He was gazing at George when he said it.

"Sounds great," she responded, blushing.

"We should reach Rainbow Cay in about twenty minutes," Kurt told them. "It's just across the strait. By the way, there's a buffet laid out in the cabin, in case you want a snack. Dinner's not till seven tonight."

"Thanks, Kurt," Bess said as he waved and walked over to another group of guests. "He likes you, George, I can tell."

"Will you stop it, Bess?" George said. "I admire him. He's a great athlete."

"And a world-class hunk," Bess said, giggling.

"Actually, I kind of feel sorry for him," Nancy said. "Being an employee at a health spa when you used to be a world-class athlete and movie star is kind of a comedown. He must be totally frustrated."

"Let's check out the buffet," Bess said, getting up and stretching. "I'm starved."

"I seem to remember that you ate on the plane," George commented.

"Ick. Don't remind me," Bess said, making a face. "Are you guys coming?"

Nancy and George followed Bess below to the cabin. Other guests were standing around the buffet table, filling their plates and chatting.

"See that tall lady over there—the one with the gold silk top?" Bess whispered to her friends. "That's Helen MacArthur, the editor of *Savoir Faire*."

"There's Sadie Thomas," George said, pointing to an attractive redhead holding a stemmed glass. "She looks better in person than on screen, don't you think?"

"She does," Bess agreed as she piled pasta salad on her plate. "And, oh, wow—isn't that Morgana Ricci, the billionaire shipping heiress?"

"Which one?" Nancy asked.

"With the frosted hair and big diamond bracelet," Bess replied.

George gasped. "Those diamonds must be worth a fortune!"

"Excuse me," Nancy said, trying to reach around a tall, thin young woman who was standing in front of the silverware. Unlike the other guests, she didn't look like a celebrity. She was wearing no makeup as far as Nancy could tell.

Her black hair was cut simply, in no particular style, and her flowered dress didn't flatter her. "Could I get a fork?"

"Oh, sorry!" the young woman said, jumping back. "I guess I was in the way." She was obviously shy and spoke with an accent.

"That's okay," Nancy said, giving her a warm smile. "Are you from Australia? I couldn't help noticing the accent."

"New Zealand, actually. I'm Maura McDaniel," she said, offering her hand to Nancy.

"I'm Nancy Drew," Nancy replied. "And these are my friends, George Fayne and Bess Marvin."

"G'day," Maura said, taking them in with her clear blue eyes. "Are you all famous? I guess you must be, if you're here," she added, blushing.

"Um, no. We're not famous at all," Nancy said, not wanting to say why they'd been invited. "We're friends of Martika. How about you?"

"Oh, me?" Maura seemed surprised at the question. "I won a contest. Coming here was the prize. Isn't that amazing? Never won anything in my life before." She let out a nervous giggle. "Oh, well. I'm looking forward to creating a 'new me.' That's what the Cloud Nine brochure said."

Nancy couldn't help feeling sad for the young woman. She didn't seem to have a lot of confidence in herself. Maybe a week at Cloud Nine *would* do her good, Nancy thought.

Just then the ship's horn sounded, and the

motor slowed. "Are we there already?" Bess asked, surprised. "Let's go on deck and see."

They all went back outside to stand at the rail. Straight ahead of them was Rainbow Cay, an emerald green speck of an island rising straight out of the sea.

Nancy could see a small harbor, where a handful of Windsurfers were gliding across the waves. Beyond the dock the island rose sharply in a steep, terraced hillside. A twisting drive lined with royal palms led up to what appeared to be the main building of the resort, a pink stucco fantasy with lots of windows and crisp white awnings. As the boat drew nearer, Nancy could see tennis courts and smaller buildings surrounding the main one.

"Most of the guests arrived earlier today," Kurt Yeager explained to the group gathered at the rail. "That's so all of you can make a grand entrance." The small crowd of celebrities laughed at Kurt's little joke. Nancy couldn't help thinking that he made an excellent host.

The yacht pulled up to the dock slowly. On land, a festive parade of motorized carts linked together like a train waited to take the guests and their luggage up to the main house.

Cutting a straight line up the hill from the dock to the main house was a staircase. It looked like a tough climb on a hot afternoon. Nancy was glad they were getting a ride.

The girls went ashore and took seats in a cart while Cloud Nine staffers attended to the baggage. As they rode up the hill, marveling at the spectacular views of the strait and St. Thomas in the distance, Kurt stood up in the front cart and addressed them over a small loudspeaker.

"Folks, I just want to show you some of our facilities as we go by. Over there," he said, pointing to the left of the main building, "is our swimming complex. We've got a big fresh-water pool for you lap swimmers, a saltwater pool, and three hot tubs. One of our water aerobics teachers was in the last Olympics. In fact, we've got more sports professionals on our staff than they have at any of the Christina Adams spas," he announced good-naturedly.

This drew an appreciative laugh from the guests, Nancy included. Christina Adams spas were the most famous in the world.

When the train of carts turned back toward the right side of the island, Kurt said, "We're passing our tennis courts now. Two-time U.S. Open winner Paul Flores is our instructor. He teaches the mental game as well as the physical. Our workout center and exercise studios are beyond the courts. High- and low-impact aerobics, strength and alignment, yoga, step classes, body sculpting, one-on-one training—you name it. We've also got every kind of training machine you could possibly imagine, plus biofeedback, nutritional counseling, hypnotherapy, stress reduction, and sports medicine."

The train of carts stopped for a moment to let two joggers in bright blue Cloud Nine spandex shorts cross the road in front of them. When it started up again, Kurt went on. "The health and beauty building is connected to the workout center by a covered walkway. That's where you go for massages, hairstyling, makeovers, facials, manicures and pedicures—the works."

Nancy glanced at Bess and George. They seemed as impressed as she was.

"What you can't see from this side of the island," Kurt went on, "is our magnificent swimming beach. It's on our south shore, behind the main house. It is completely secluded because Cloud Nine is the only resort or house of any kind on Rainbow Cay."

A round of applause answered him. Nancy couldn't help thinking that if Kurt didn't like his job, he was doing a terrific job of hiding it.

Kurt kept pointing things out as the cars swung around one sharp turn after another. "Below us, near where we docked, is our other beach. The surf's calmer there. That's where you'll find our scuba shack. We've got snorkeling, diving, an underwater trail along the reef, sailboats, jet skis, Windsurfers—and instructors to help you with everything."

Just then the carts reached the top of the hill

and came to a stop. Martika Sawyer, radiant in a pink pastel caftan, was standing on the steps of the resort to greet them. Her raven hair glistened in the sunlight, and her ice blue eyes sparkled. Nancy had to admit that she was as beautiful as she appeared to be on her magazine covers.

A few photographers were standing around her, ready to shoot Martika and the new celebrity arrivals. Nancy supposed they were members of the press covering the opening of Cloud Nine.

"Welcome, welcome, welcome!" Martika gushed, blowing kisses to her guests. "I'm thrilled that you're here. We're going to have a fabulous time together."

Nancy noticed that Martika and Kurt barely nodded to each other. As he stepped out of the cart, he seemed to have lost all of his energy. He backed away, leaving Martika to her friends and admirers.

A prosperous-looking middle-aged man with silver hair joined Martika on the steps. "I'd like you all to meet Preston Winchell, my silent partner." She gave the man's arm a squeeze.

"Hello, everyone," he said with a smile and a nod. "Hope you all have a great time."

"There, you see?" Martika said. "He's not so silent after all!"

Everyone laughed.

Joining Martika on her other side was a tall, handsome man with dark hair and blue eyes almost identical to Martika's. He held a pair of binoculars in one hand. Martika now slipped her arm through his and introduced him. "And this is my brother, Derek," she explained. "If you have any questions and can't find me, he'll be happy to help you. Won't you, Derek?"

"Thrilled," Derek echoed, smiling and nodding to the guests. Nancy detected a hint of sarcasm in his tone.

Just then Derek's expression changed to a frown as he peered into the distance. "There seems to be another boat approaching," he said. He lifted his binoculars to his eyes. "We aren't expecting any more arrivals, are we, Martika?"

"Give me those," Martika said quickly, taking the binoculars from him and training them on the large yacht that was now entering the harbor.

Suddenly Martika gasped and dropped the binoculars.

"What is it, Martika?" Preston Winchell asked, taking one of her hands in his.

"I'll kill her!" she said, her eyes wild with fury as she stared out at the harbor. "I'll murder that woman if it's the last thing I do!"

Chapter

Two

BEFORE ANYONE could react, Martika made a dash for the steps that led down to the dock.

"Martika! Wait!" Derek called as he took off after her. The photographers scurried close behind. Everyone else was too startled to move, but soon began talking about what had happened.

"Folks," Kurt called, climbing the steps to the porch in two giant leaps. "I'll show you all to the lobby," he said, doing his best to cover for Martika.

Nancy had stooped down to pick up the binoculars Martika had dropped. She trained them on the harbor below.

The newly arrived yacht had anchored offshore, and a motor launch was now pulling away from it and moving toward the dock. A uniformed man was at the wheel with just one

13

passenger—a willowy woman in a white sundress, holding a hand to her hat to keep it from blowing off in the wind.

"Come on," Nancy said to Bess and George. "Let's see what's up."

She took off down the steps, with Bess and George right behind her. A few of the other guests decided to go, too, including Helen MacArthur, the magazine editor. Most of them followed Kurt Yeager, buzzing about all the commotion.

At the bottom of the long flight of steps, Martika stood on the dock glaring at the motor launch. Derek was behind her with his hands on her shoulders, clearly trying to calm her.

"That woman in the boat," Bess said, short of breath as she joined Nancy and George on the dock several feet off to the side of Martika. "I recognize her from her ads—it's Christina Adams."

"The health spa queen?" George whispered. "But she's Martika's biggest competitor. What's she doing here?"

"Good question, George," Nancy said. The motor launch docked at the wharf, and a staffer reached out to give Christina Adams a hand up.

"Dear, dear Martika!" Christina said, going right up to the model. She planted a kiss on Martika's cheek. Martika stood, rigid with anger, as the photographers' cameras snapped. "I'm so sorry to crash your little party like this, but would you believe it, my boat developed engine trouble just as we were passing! Isn't that awful? I'm sure they'll have it fixed quickly, but until then it looks as if I'm stranded."

Christina removed her hat to show off her sun-streaked honey blond hair. She batted her long eyelashes at the newspeople. Martika continued to stand there with her hands on her hips, apparently too furious to speak.

Nancy knew a little of the history between the two women. Christina Adams's salons and spas were legendary. In opening up her resort, Martika was challenging Christina's empire—which wasn't likely to make Christina happy. Now here she was, crashing Martika's opening.

Behind Martika, Nancy heard Derek mutter, "Uh-oh, trouble in paradise."

"You *are* going to ask me to stay, aren't you?" Christina asked, acting like a little lost waif. "I promise I'll be quiet as a mouse," she said, giggling lightly. "And, oh, what a lovely place you've got here! I'm so happy for you! I'm sure you're going to be a great success." Once again she kissed the flushed Martika on the cheek, then waved to the photographers.

"She could stay on her boat, you know," Nancy heard Derek whisper in Martika's ear.

Martika shook her head and seemed to come

out of her daze. "No, no, Derek. Of course Christina must stay with us," she said, giving her rival a plastic smile. "I'm sure you'll be very happy here. And who knows—you might even pick up a few pointers about how to run a world-class spa."

Having had the last word, Martika marched back up the steps at a rapid pace. Derek remained with the press and Christina as the train of carts approached to take them back up the hill.

Nancy didn't want to wait. Signaling for Bess and George to follow, she took off after Martika, catching her about halfway up the steps.

"Martika!" she said. The gorgeous model turned. "I'm Nancy Drew," Nancy said, extending her hand. "And these are my friends, Bess and George," she added when Bess and George caught up.

"Nancy!" Martika said, suddenly seeming to relax. She shook hands with all three girls and gave them a dazzling smile. "I'm sorry you had to witness what just happened. I can't believe that woman had the nerve to show up here! She's trying to ruin my opening."

"I thought it was very nice of you to invite her to stay," Nancy offered.

"What else could I do?" Martika asked, sighing. "The press was watching. It wouldn't have looked very good if I'd refused. What I really wanted to do, though, was strangle her."

Martika gave a sad little laugh. "Just kidding, of course. But, you know, it isn't easy going into a business like this. It wouldn't take much to wreck everything I've set up. And I want everything to be perfect. Preston Winchell, my financial backer, is here, and I just know Christina would love to steal him and his support from me."

"I think she has a lot of nerve to just show up like she did," Bess volunteered.

"And how convenient that her boat had engine trouble right here at Rainbow Cay," George added.

"It does look calculated," Nancy agreed. "Martika, could Christina's arrival have anything to do with the problems you wanted to tell me about?"

Martika peered up and down the stairs, then said, "Since you mentioned it, let's talk. I know the perfect place."

She turned off the stairway and led them down a path lined with blooming bougainvillea. It twisted below the tennis courts and ended in a lovely secluded garden enclosed by a brick wall. Two frangipani trees bordered the entrance, and inside there were stone benches set amid perfectly tended beds of flowers and herbs. The air was piquant with their aroma.

"It's so peaceful here," Nancy said, breathing in the smell of a combination of sage, basil, clove, and mint.

"This is where we're suggesting people come to meditate. We'll try to attend to the soul as well as the body at Cloud Nine," Martika explained.

They sat down on the benches surrounding a small fountain. "You were going to explain why you sent for me," Nancy prompted.

"I've been receiving threats," Martika said, focusing only on Nancy. "Notes warning me not to open the resort. Of course I ignored them—nothing's going to stop me from making Cloud Nine a success. Still, I want to find out who sent them and what the person is planning."

"What about the police?" Nancy asked.

"Out of the question," Martika said. "Can you picture this place crawling with the St. Thomas police? The reporters and photographers would have a field day, and my grand opening would be a disaster."

Nancy understood. "Has anyone else seen the notes?" she asked.

"No one," Martika said softly.

"Not even your brother?" George asked.

"Derek?" Martika looked as though the idea of showing the notes to him was absurd. "Derek's my brother, and I love him. But he can't keep a secret."

"Could *he* have written the notes?" Nancy asked.

Martika appeared to be taken aback by the

question. "Oh, no," she said uncertainly. "At least, I don't think so. I can't imagine he'd do that to me after all I've done for him. Besides, why would he want me to fail? I'm his meal ticket—always have been."

Martika shook her head and went on, "If you ask me, Christina Adams is behind everything. I would have said so even before she pulled this latest stunt. Now I'm sure it's her."

"I'd like to see the notes," Nancy said.

"Of course," Martika said, rising. "They're in my suite. I want to show them to you."

As they walked back up the hill to the main building, the conversation turned to other things. "I've always loved your photos," Bess said. "You have so many different looks. How do you do it?"

"Oh, that's mostly the photographers' and stylists' genius, not mine," Martika said modestly.

"You know which photo spread of yours I really loved?" Bess asked. "The one you did with the snake. It was incredible. But weren't you scared?"

"Scared?" Martika repeated as she led them into the lobby where the guests were getting to know one another and checking out the boutiques. "Not at all. I love animals, including snakes. The snake in the spread was my pet boa, Squeeze."

19

"Squeeze?" George repeated. "It sounds dangerous."

"Hardly," Martika said. "He wouldn't hurt a fly. Besides, I feed him well and keep him in a very strong cage in my suite." Leading them down a softly lit, white-carpeted corridor, she added, "Would you like to meet him?"

"I'll pass," Bess said a little shakily.

"Oh, don't be silly, he's perfectly wonderful. He loves people, and he's not at all slimy or dangerous," Martika insisted as she stopped at the door to her suite and unlocked it.

The outer chamber was a combination office and sitting room, with a sliding glass door that opened onto a private patio. Set against one wall were a large white lacquered desk and a huge bookshelf. "The notes are in my desk," Martika said. "But come say hello to Squeeze first."

Opening another door, she led them into her living quarters. The entire suite was decorated in pastels: peach walls and a powder blue ceiling that echoed the blue of the sky. A king-size canopy bed was centered on the far wall. It was covered with plump, patterned pillows. Beside it was a night table with a graceful bird-of-paradise bouquet.

They passed the open door into Martika's bathroom. "Wow, what an incredible setup!" Bess said, peeking inside.

"Go on in and look," Martika offered, and the girls filed in. There was an enormous Jacuzzi with whirlpool jets, a sauna, and towel warmer. On the dressing table was an unbelievable variety of cosmetics and beauty aids.

Martika reached for a crystal bottle. "See these fragrances? Essence of sage, mint, rosemary, orange blossom, and clove. They're all made at our beauty center from plants that grow in the herb garden and other places on the island." She unscrewed the top and dabbed a bit behind Bess's ear. "It's lavender—my favorite."

"Thanks!" Bess said.

"Come," Martika said after a moment. "Let me introduce you to Squeeze." She led them out of the dressing room and back into the bedroom.

"I see his cage," George said, pointing to a Plexiglas structure in the corner that was more a tropical habitat than a cage. Inside it were plants and a small bubbling fountain.

"I don't see a snake," Nancy said, examining the cage. "Unless he's hiding."

"He'd be too big to hide," Bess said.

"Squeeze?" Martika called out, searching the cage with her eyes. "Here, Squeeze."

Her voice rose and reflected her panic when it became obvious that the cage was empty. "He's not here!" Martika said, aghast. "And the cage door is closed. Someone must have let him out."

21

Bess's eyes grew round, and Nancy circled around to the back of the cage to search for the snake.

"Where could he be?" Martika asked.

Then they heard a piercing scream from down the hall. It was all the answer they needed.

Chapter

Three

"Squeeze!" Martika sped out of her suite and down the hall in the direction of the shrieks. Nancy and the girls followed close behind.

The screams were coming from a guest room around the corner from Martika's suite, where the door was open. Inside was a plump, middle-aged woman standing on a chair, clearly petrified. On the floor below her was one of the largest snakes Nancy had ever seen.

"Squeeze!" Martika cried in relief. "Bad boy! What are you doing out of your cage?" With a single deft motion, Martika hoisted the snake over her shoulder, petting him to keep him calm. "I'm so sorry, Mrs. Smythe," she said breathlessly. "I don't know how this happened. Are you all right?"

The woman still seemed unable to speak. "Oh!

23

Oh!" was all she kept saying, as Nancy helped her down from her chair.

Martika backed away to keep the snake at some distance from Mrs. Smythe. "Squeeze is completely harmless," she added.

Mrs. Smythe found her voice. "Harmless," she gasped. She brushed the winkles out of the skirt of her dress and patted her hair into place. "It's a boa constrictor, for heaven's sake!"

"Please, Mrs. Smythe," Martika pleaded. "It was just an unfortunate accident. You were never in any danger."

Nancy led the woman to the couch and settled her there. She seemed to be quieting down a bit. "I can't imagine what my husband will say when he hears about this. He's a lawyer, you know."

Martika frowned but then said soothingly, "I promise you, dear, that by the time you leave Cloud Nine you'll want to have your picture taken with Squeeze. I did, you know. They ran a layout with the two of us in *Chic.*"

"Oh," Mrs. Smythe said, her eyes widening with interest. She breathed deeply a few times. "Well, I really doubt that—"

"And, of course, your stay at the resort will be completely complimentary," Martika interrupted. "You'll be my personal guest."

"Well . . ." Mrs. Smythe said, happier but not completely mollified.

"And I'd love to do a beauty session with you," Martika added.

This last offer seemed to touch the right button. Mrs. Smythe couldn't stop a smile from creeping across her face. "That would be nice," she said, then focused on the snake again. "Is he really tame?" She inched forward to peer closer at the creature she'd been so terrified of just a few minutes earlier.

"Completely," Martika assured her. "Why don't I give you an autographed copy of one of the shots I did with him?"

"Oh, would you?" Mrs. Smythe cooed. "That would be lovely!"

"Well, *you've* been lovely," Martika said graciously. "And you won't say a word about all this, will you?"

"Oh, no." Mrs. Smythe was blushing now.

"Really?" Martika said, backing toward the door. "That would be so helpful. You're so understanding, Mrs. Smythe. Now, I hope you'll promise to sit with me at dinner?"

"Oh, yes. Of course, I will," Mrs. Smythe said. She waved goodbye as Martika and the girls retreated to the safety of the model's suite. There Martika opened the cage door and slid the snake back inside. That done, she heaved a sigh of relief and collapsed into a white wicker chair.

"That was incredible, the way you turned her

around," George said admiringly as she sat down on the loveseat.

"Really!" Bess agreed, taking a seat next to George. "I was sure she'd be calling her lawyer husband."

"Well, thanks, girls," Martika said, laughing at the thought of it. "I guess I can still turn on the charm when I have to."

"I'll say," Bess said. "Boy, Squeeze sure is scary, though." She was staring at the cage, where the snake had curled up for a nap.

Nancy went over to it. Something had been bothering her about what had just happened, and now she knew what it was. "The door of your suite was locked, Martika," she said. "Your terrace door, too. Right?"

The model nodded.

"So the question is, who besides you has a key?"

"The housekeeping staff has a master key. But the maids are too afraid to go near Squeeze's cage," she said. "Besides that key, only my brother, Derek, has one," Martika said. "But he wouldn't try to sabotage me. He's capable of pulling a prank now and then, but not this week. He knows how much this opening means to me."

Nancy didn't say anything.

"Derek is careless," Martika went on. "He probably left his key lying around somewhere and somebody got hold of it."

"Like who?" Nancy asked.

Martika raised her hands and then dropped them. "I have no idea. Maybe someone on my staff is a spy for Christina Adams. She's got every reason to want to ruin me. If Cloud Nine is a success, if it gets great write-ups, if Preston Winchell decides to back more Martika Sawyer resorts . . ."

"I see what you mean," Nancy said, nodding thoughtfully. "You could be a real threat to her."

"She's been alone at the top of the spa business for so long," Martika explained. "No one has even come close to challenging her. I'm a model, and to Christina a model has no brains or business sense. But when I got Preston Winchell to back me, she was really shaken. Christina was trying to get him to invest in her spas, but he put his money behind me instead."

"Why would Christina need outside backing?" Nancy asked.

"Because she's deep in debt," Martika told her. "She constantly borrows to open new resorts, and now every penny she makes goes to pay off what she owes. If I'm successful and open up a few more places like this, she could lose enough customers to bankrupt her."

"I see," Nancy said.

"On the other hand, if my opening week is a flop, and the magazines and newspapers report it that way, Preston Winchell could decide it's too risky to keep backing me. And if he pulls out, it would be impossible to replace his money fast enough to stay open. If Christina can spoil this week for me, it could mean all the difference between success and failure."

"And that's why you're so sure she's the one who wrote the notes," Nancy said.

"Don't you think so?" Martika asked.

"I don't know," Nancy said. "She certainly didn't have time to let Squeeze out." Nancy was sympathetic but practical. "I'm afraid we've got to consider other suspects, too. What about Kurt Yeager? Excuse me for being so frank, but I heard you two had a pretty nasty breakup. True?"

Martika was silent for a moment before nodding and answering, "Yes, it's true. Kurt and I were very much in love at first. But then—I don't know—things went sour somehow. He couldn't take my success. After his movie career flopped, he became irrational and would fly into insane rages for no reason. It was like he became a different person. I never stopped caring about him really, which is why I offered him the job here. I figured he was pretty low and needed a boost."

"Maybe he hasn't forgiven you," Nancy suggested. "Maybe he's carrying a grudge, and this is his way of taking it out on you."

"I suppose it's possible," Martika said slowly. "He always was jealous, and I do know he resents me because I dropped him. But I just can't believe he'd go this far."

"One thing's for sure," Nancy said. "Both Kurt and Derek knew where Squeeze was. Is there anyone else here who might have something against you?"

"Not that I know of," Martika said. "But I'll give it some thought."

"Now, if I could see those notes," Nancy said.

"Of course," Martika replied, leading them back into the outer room of the suite. Martika riffled through the drawers of her desk and pulled out two pieces of folded paper.

"They both arrived in the mail with a Saint Thomas postmark," Martika told Nancy. "I know Christina's been sailing around the Caribbean for the last couple of weeks, so she easily could have mailed them from there. So could anyone who works here."

Nancy examined the letters, which had clearly been printed by a computer. One said: "If you open Cloud Nine, its going to rain on your parade."

The other note was similar in tone: "Call off your opening, Martika. This warning is from a frend."

"The person can't spell at all," Nancy commented. "Which tells us something, at least. Also the person says he or she is a friend."

"Ha!" Bess broke in. "Some friend."

"I'm so glad you're here, Nancy," Martika said, putting a hand on her shoulder. "I'm sure you'll get to the bottom of this. You just have to!" Nancy could see the desperation in Martika's face. "This place means everything to me."

"I'll do my best," Nancy assured her.

"Well, you'd better go unpack," Martika said. "Here, let me show you where your suite is." She led them to the door, then stopped short.

A folded piece of paper lay near a chair beside the door. Nancy hadn't noticed it before.

Martika bent down to retrieve it. Opening it with trembling hands, she studied it for a moment. "I was afraid of this," she said, handing the sheet of paper to Nancy.

Nancy read the message out loud, her voice tight. "'I mean bisness. This is only the beginning. Close down now—or die!'"

Chapter

Four

NANCY EXAMINED the note closely. "I think we have to take this threat seriously, Martika," she said. "You called me down here to help, and I'm going to do my best to find the person responsible. But the person has now threatened your life, and I think you should call in the police now."

Martika sighed with frustration. "I already told you, that's out of the question," she said.

"Well, then," Nancy persisted, "at least put your security staff on alert, and have a bodyguard with you at all times."

Martika lifted her hands in dismay. "Are you kidding?" she asked. "How would that look? Me walking around with some big hulk in a uniform!"

"What about someone who knows martial arts?" Nancy suggested. "A woman, maybe. She would draw less attention. People would just think she was your personal assistant."

"Nancy," Martika said, "your job is to find out who wrote these notes. I can take care of myself. Besides, whoever it is, I'm sure the death threat isn't serious. The person just wants to ruin Cloud Nine."

Nancy shook her head slowly—she was getting nowhere with Martika. If anything more happened, she'd have to try again to convince her to go to the police.

"Come on, you two," she said to Bess and George. "We'd better get unpacked. It's getting close to dinnertime."

The girls rose and Martika pointed them down the hallway toward the lobby. "You're on the second floor at the far end of the building. Suite Two Twenty-five. See you at dinner," she said. "And thanks again. I'm glad you're all here— now I don't feel so alone." Martika gave them a little wave before reentering her suite.

The girls had to pass through the lobby. There they stopped to examine a bulletin board. "Oh, look!" George said excitedly. "Kurt's giving that body-sculpting demonstration he told us about. I think we should go."

Nancy read the handwritten notice. "Body scupting demonstration by Kurt Yeager. Today from five-thirty to six. Fitness studio."

"It's five-forty now," Bess pointed out, glancing at the clock on the lobby wall. "If we hurry, we can still catch half of it."

"I'm into it," George said. "What about you, Nan? After all, he did invite us."

"Sure," Nancy said. She took down the note and put it into the pocket of her white jeans. "Evidence," she explained as they headed outside and down the path, following signs to the workout center. "Body *scupting?* Maybe it's just coincidence, but Kurt Yeager sure can't spell."

"You don't really think— I mean, he's so nice," Bess said.

"So gorgeous, you mean," Nancy corrected. "Since when are gorgeous guys innocent?"

Bess frowned, but none of them said anything.

The white gravel path they were on ended at the workout center. They entered the skylighted lobby where there were plush chairs, a health food snack bar, and a small shop crowded with racks of colorful workout clothes. The attendant at the front desk directed them down a long corridor to the exercise studio where Kurt was giving his demonstration.

Nancy nudged the door open and admired the highly polished wood floor and floor-to-ceiling mirrors. Kurt Yeager was raising and lowering two ten-pound hand weights to the strains of hard-driving rock. He wore biking shorts and no shirt. From the sidelines, a dozen women were watching him admiringly.

"Now I can die completely happy," Bess said with a sigh. George rolled her eyes at Bess's comment. When Kurt saw them and flashed them a blinding smile, Nancy saw George redden.

The demonstration went on for a few more minutes, with Kurt showing how to work various muscles in the arms and back using the weights. He finished with a series of stomach crunches to strengthen the abdominals. Then he sprang up and grinned. "That's all for today, ladies. Thanks for coming, and sorry I was late getting here. Tomorrow afternoon I'll be leading a body-sculpting class. Hope to see you all here."

After chatting with a few stragglers, Kurt wandered over to the three girls. "Glad you made it," he said.

"Sorry we were late," George apologized.

"Kurt, you said you were late, too. What held you up?" Nancy asked.

"Oh, I had to get the celebrities settled— Martika's orders. The way she figures it, all the paying guests will get a thrill from hanging out with stars. Besides, the press will focus on the celebrities. So if they're happy, the write-ups will be good. So keeping them happy is my job."

"Are they happy so far?" George asked.

Kurt laughed. "Some of them can be pretty hard to please. Morgana Ricci, the shipping heiress, was furious about her eating regimen. She's limited to twelve hundred calories a day, and she's not happy."

"How did you handle her?" Nancy asked.

"I told her our nutritionists would be happy to devise a more flexible diet for her," he said, giving them a wink.

"Morgana Ricci really could stand to take off a few pounds," Bess chimed in. "Of course, who couldn't?" she added, biting her lip.

"Meaning you?" Kurt asked, surprised. "You look great. But your point is well taken. There's hardly anybody who couldn't be in a little better shape."

"Seeing to all those people must have taken forever," Nancy said. She was wondering if Kurt had had time to let Squeeze out of his cage and push the note under Martika's door.

"Only about an hour," Kurt said. As he walked them back to the main house, Nancy made a mental note to cross-check his story with the celebrity guests.

The girls went up to their suite, which was a smaller, simpler version of Martika's, but with the same great views.

"Hey, look!" Bess said, going over to one of the beds. "There are gift packs for us."

George checked out her bed and opened the pack. "A Cloud Nine water bottle with straw, fanny pack, T-shirt, and—oh, neat—a tube of Cloud Nine organic moisturizer."

After going through their gifts, the girls began to freshen up and change.

"Our very own Jacuzzi," Bess called out from the bathroom.

"I figure I'll need a good soak after working out," George said, peeking in the doorway. She stopped in front of a dresser near the bathroom door. "Hey," she said, picking up a sheet of paper. "We have to fill out these forms for our personal fitness consultations."

"After dinner, George," Nancy said. "If we don't hurry, we're going to be late."

As soon as they were ready, they made their way down to the main dining room, which was already crowded with what seemed to be about two hundred guests.

The room, which overlooked the back patio, was furnished formally, French chateau style. At one end, on a raised dais, was Martika's table. She sat in the center seat, flanked by Helen MacArthur, editor of *Savoir Faire,* and Preston Winchell. On the financier's other side was a beaming Mrs. Smythe.

The maitre d' showed the girls to a table, and Nancy found herself sitting next to Christina

Adams. She suspected that Martika had arranged it that way so that she could keep an eye on Christina.

Kurt Yeager was also at their table, next to George, and Derek was sitting beside Bess. Martika's brother seized the opportunity to flirt outrageously with Bess, while she giggled at everything he whispered in her ear.

When all the guests were assembled, Martika stood and tapped her knife on her water glass. The diners quieted down, and Martika began to speak.

"I'd like to welcome you all again to Cloud Nine," she said warmly. "I hope you have a week to remember for the rest of your lives."

After a brief but spirited round of applause, she continued, "I know you are here to relax and enjoy yourselves, and of course Cloud Nine is the perfect place to do that. But you are also here for life-changing reasons, too—be they physical, mental, or spiritual. You'll be following a personalized regimen of workouts and treatments designed just for you. And we promise to do everything in our power to help you."

Martika sat down to more applause as the waiters served the vegetable pâté appetizer. Nancy knew that all the meals at Cloud Nine were planned and prepared to be nutritious and low in calories. One bite of the pâté told her that she could count on their tasting delicious, too. After the first course came filet of sole Florentine and a salad, topped off by lemon sorbet for dessert.

Turned out in a dramatic green dress, Christina kept casting sly glances at Martika's table and, particularly, at Preston Winchell. Every time he noticed her, she smiled bewitchingly. It was obvious to Nancy that she was already trying to woo Winchell and his wallet away from Martika.

When she wasn't eyeing the financier, Christina gossiped mercilessly about Martika. "Did you know that her real name is Sawin, not Sawyer?" Christina said at one point. "They had to change their last name because her father was involved in a stock scandal of some kind."

Nancy casually mentioned Martika's boa constrictor, trying to get a reaction out of the woman. If Christina was behind the release of the snake, she hid it well. No surprise registered on her pretty face.

At one point Nancy caught sight of Maura McDaniel, the young woman she'd met on the boat ride from St. Thomas. Sitting at a table with Morgana Ricci and Sadie Thomas, Maura stood out because she was so plain. Not only that, she seemed miserable. Nobody was paying the slightest bit of attention to her.

Excusing herself after dessert, Nancy went

over to say hello to Maura. "How are you doing?" she asked the New Zealander.

Maura shrugged lightly. "Oh, all right, I guess," she said, and then looked away. "I've been a bit homesick, to tell the truth," she finally admitted.

"Really?" Nancy asked. "But this is such a beautiful place—" Nancy stopped in midsentence, realizing that it might be all the beauty that was making Maura feel insecure.

"It *is* lovely," Maura agreed. "But I miss my home. I miss my dad 'specially. He died a few months ago."

"Oh. I'm sorry," Nancy said sympathetically.

"I'm all alone now," Maura said with a sigh, but then she grinned. "Maybe when I've been transformed into a 'new me' I'll find somebody, eh?"

"I'm sure you will," Nancy said reassuringly. Privately, she thought Maura needed a massive injection of self-confidence to attract people. "Well, I'd better get back to my table. See you tomorrow?"

"I hope so," Maura said. "You're very nice to come over and talk to me. Nancy, is it?"

Nancy turned back to her own table just in time to see Derek getting up. With a quick glance to make sure Martika wasn't checking on him, he left the room. Nancy couldn't help thinking that he was acting guilty about something. On a hunch, she followed him out into the lobby and then down the hall, keeping a safe distance between them.

Derek made a beeline for Martika's suite. When he reached the door, Nancy ducked into an alcove, where she could secretly watch him. He pulled something out of his pocket and jimmied the door open with it. It appeared to be a pick. Maybe someone *had* stolen his key, she thought.

Derek went inside, and before the self-closing door swung shut behind him, Nancy got a hand on the knob.

Holding the door slightly ajar, Nancy could see a small segment of the room, one that included Martika's white-lacquered desk. As it turned out, she didn't need to see more of the suite because Derek went directly to the desk. Using the pick again, he opened the top drawer and pulled out a large checkbook. As he opened it, he picked up the phone and punched in seven numbers. No area code, Nancy thought. So he had to be calling somewhere in the U.S. Virgin Islands.

"Hello?" Derek said, tearing a check out of the book and writing on it. "It's me, Derek. Now wait a minute, don't get hot under the collar. I'll get you the money I owe you. I'm writing out a Cloud Nine check right now. There'll be more soon. Believe me—"

The conversation lasted for a minute longer,

with the person on the other end doing most of the talking. Finally Derek hung up, folded the check in half, and put it in his pocket.

Nancy could barely believe what she'd just seen. Unless she was mistaken, Derek Sawyer was stealing from his own sister!

Chapter

Five

NANCY WATCHED, rooted to the spot, as Derek returned the checkbook to the drawer. While he was bending over to do so, she let the door close silently and ran toward the lobby. Just before she got there she saw a ladies' room and went in, staying until she was reasonably sure Derek had passed.

By the time she returned to the dining room, Bess and George were getting up from their chairs. "Guess what, Nan?" Bess said excitedly. "During dinner Derek asked me to go dancing with him tomorrow night!"

"Are you sure you're going to feel like dancing after a day of workouts?" Nancy asked.

"Oh, don't worry about me," Bess said. "I'll be fine. I'm going to lose five pounds, too. By tomorrow night I may even have sweated them off. Then I can spend the rest of the week eating and hanging out!"

Nancy laughed as they made their way upstairs to their suite. "But I think there's something you should know about Derek."

"He's tall, dark, and handsome," Bess said. "What else is there to know?"

When they were inside their suite, Nancy told her friends what she had just seen.

Bess was sobered by the news. "Well, at least I can try to find out what he's up to," she offered.

"Great," Nancy said.

"Speaking of men," Bess said, turning to George, "tell Nan about your big date."

"Big date?" Nancy repeated.

"She's teasing," George said to Nancy. "Kurt asked me to play tennis with him. He has an hour free before lunch. So when I make up my schedule in the morning, I'll work it around that. I know I want to try water aerobics and run the par course. Maybe some snorkeling, too. Of course, if you need me for any investigating, Nan . . ."

"We'll see," Nancy said. "In any case, Kurt's one of our main suspects, so don't get too dreamy eyed. Do try to draw him out about Martika, though."

"Gotcha. Serve and volley, but no love," George quipped. "Do you seriously think it's Kurt, though? I mean, just because he can't spell?"

"I would have said yes until a few minutes ago," Nancy replied. "Now I've got to consider Derek, too. Of course, it doesn't make sense that he'd try to ruin his sister. But we know he's stealing from her. So there's definitely more to him than meets the eye."

"Isn't there always?" Bess said with a sigh. "Why can't a gorgeous guy just be gorgeous?"

Bess yawned. "I'm exhausted," she said, stretching. "What time is it?"

George checked her watch and said, "Almost ten. Do you realize we were up at five-thirty this morning in River Heights?"

"Well, if I'm getting up at seven, I'm going to bed right now," Bess said, heading for the bathroom. "I've got a monster day ahead of me. How about you, George?"

"I'm with you," she said, getting up. "Nan?"

"I'll prowl around awhile first," Nancy said. "My mind is racing a mile a minute still, and I don't think I could sleep if I tried."

"Sorting out the suspects already?" George asked, stopping short of the bathroom.

"Uh-huh." After saying good night, Nancy went downstairs to the lobby and out the rear doors to the patio. It was dotted with wrought-iron tables and chairs and ended about a hundred feet from the edge of the cliff. Off to the left was a gazebo, perfectly placed for watching the secluded beach below.

In all, there were three sets of stairs leading down to the shore—one toward the middle of the patio and one at either end. All along the stone railing, people stood in small groups or pairs gazing out at the crashing surf and star-studded sky. Nancy joined them, struck by the beauty of the scene.

"Hi, there." Nancy wheeled around to see Martika approaching, wearing a white blouse with billowing sleeves and a flowing dark skirt. "I went to your suite, and your friends said you'd gone for a walk. Glad I found you."

"Did you want to talk to me about anything in particular?" Nancy asked.

"Lots of things," Martika said, slipping an arm through Nancy's and leading her toward the set of stairs farthest from the gazebo. "I was just going for my nightly walk on the beach. Will you please come along so we can talk?"

"Great," Nancy said, raising her eyes to the sky. The moon was full and orange, with knife-like clouds racing across it.

"I love walking on the beach at night," Martika said as they started down the stairs. "It helps me unwind. I've been so busy getting ready for the opening. And with all the threats—" she added in a whisper.

"I can imagine," Nancy said sympathetically.

The steps down to the beach were lit with little multicolored electric lanterns. Nancy noticed that the cliff wasn't terribly high or steep, but it had lots of rugged outcroppings of rocks.

"You've done a fantastic job designing this place," Nancy said admiringly. "I can't imagine it won't be successful."

Martika put a hand on Nancy's arm. "It'll be successful if *you* are," she said.

Nancy nodded. "By the way," she began, "Kurt was late for his body-sculpting demonstration this afternoon. He says he was taking care of the celebrity guests. But he might have had time to let Squeeze out and drop that note."

"I really doubt that, Nancy," Martika replied. Then she frowned. "What bothers me is that he was late for that demonstration. Kurt may be a problem. His attitude couldn't be worse."

"He seems to have a great attitude to me," Nancy said.

"Maybe it's only when I'm around that he has an attitude," Martika said.

"One thing's for sure—his spelling is terrible," Nancy remarked. She took Kurt's notice out of her pocket and showed it to Martika.

Martika's eyes grew round with surprise. "So it *was* Kurt who wrote those notes. Maybe he's in cahoots with Christina. I had a funny feeling it was a mistake to give him a job, but I ignored it. I guess he's never forgiven me for breaking up with him."

"Wait a minute," Nancy said, calmly laying a hand on Martika's shoulder. "This isn't exactly concrete proof that he's guilty. Someone may just be trying to make him appear that way."

Martika blinked, taking it in. "I see," she said, nodding slowly. "Anyway, I can't very well fire him in the middle of my opening week. How would it look?"

Martika stopped at a landing halfway down and leaned against the rail. The breeze rustled her coal black hair.

"Tell me about Derek," Nancy said. "I know you don't think it's him, but still . . ."

"Derek? He's a gambler who never wins. I've been bailing him out ever since our father died. We lost our mother when Derek was just a baby, and Dad raised us. Things were hard. I don't know how much you know about my past."

"Nothing at all," Nancy admitted. "I don't read celebrity magazines much. That's Bess's department."

"I see. Well, at one time my dad was a big Wall Street broker. He and his brother owned their own brokerage firm. But then one day my uncle disappeared, taking all the firm's assets with him. Of course the brokerage house failed. My father made good on all the claims against it and went broke in the process. He never spoke about it when we were growing up, but I dug around and

47

found out. We were never allowed to mention my uncle around our house."

"And he changed your family name from Sawin to Sawyer?" Nancy asked.

Martika was taken aback. "How did you know that?"

"Christina," Nancy told her.

Martika frowned. "That woman is always spreading dirt about me," she complained.

"Where did your uncle go?" Nancy asked, getting back to the subject.

"I have no idea," Martika said. "Out of the country, I presume. In any case, we were poor from then on. I started modeling to support us, and Derek started sponging off me. Since Dad died a couple of years ago, Derek's gone to pot. Oh, he looks good, but he can't hold down a job. He always comes to me for money, and I always give it to him. But I told him last week the party was over, that he'd have to earn his keep by helping me with Cloud Nine."

"I see," Nancy said. "Did you know he was stealing company checks?"

Martika gave Nancy a startled look, which immediately turned to one of admiration. "You're very good, Nancy. Carson was right. I'm glad I asked you to come here."

Then she stared out at the water and sighed. "Yes, I know Derek has been writing checks and forging my name. It's not the sort of thing a person can get away with for very long. I've been replacing the amounts from my own savings. But as I said, I've told him it's got to stop. He's on the payroll now, and he's going to have to live on his salary. Anyway, I still don't think he'd sabotage me, since I supply him with money."

"I guess so," Nancy agreed, as they continued on down the steps. There was no one else on the beach. After they stepped off the stairs, Martika kicked off her sandals, and Nancy did the same. The sand felt powdery fine between her toes, and the air was tangy with salt. The full moon provided plenty of light and turned the waves silver.

"When I had the idea for this place," Martika said, "nobody believed I could bring it off. 'You'll never make it,' they said." She swung around gracefully and spread her arms out wide. "I'll show them all, though. This place is only the beginning for me. A few years from now I'll be the owner of a whole network of resorts all over the world." She laughed and spun around joyfully. The moonlight made her lovely face glow.

Without warning the model gasped and stopped dead in her tracks about five feet in front of Nancy.

"Something just buzzed by me!" she cried. "Did you feel it?"

"No," Nancy said, surprised. "What was it?"

"I don't know," Martika replied. She was searching all around her. "A bat, maybe."

"Are you sure?" Nancy asked. "I didn't hear anything."

"It whooshed right by me," Martika insisted. "How strange."

Nancy reached into her pocket and took out the flashlight she always carried with her. Shining it at Martika, she took hold of the model's wide sleeve. There was a neat round hole on the inner side, between the elbow and the shoulder.

Nancy put a finger through it. "Was this hole here before?" she asked Martika.

Martika peered down at it. "Why, no," she said. "But that's right where I felt the whooshing go by. While my arms were over my head, like this."

Nancy suddenly grabbed Martika by the hand and pulled her away from the water to a spot sheltered by the cliff.

"That hole was not made by a bat, Martika," she said. "It was made by a bullet. Someone just took a shot at you!"

Chapter

Six

A GUNSHOT?" MARTIKA repeated, clutching Nancy's hand. "Are you sure?"

"Pretty sure," Nancy said. "There are two holes in your sleeve, see? An entry hole and an exit hole. Both very neat."

"But I didn't hear anything, Nancy—only a light whizzing noise." The model's voice had taken on a pleading quality.

"The gun probably had a silencer on it," Nancy explained.

Martika's eyes widened and her expression froze, registering her fear.

Nancy did her best to sound soothing, even though she knew that the situation didn't warrant it. "It's okay, Martika. You're all right. But I do need to figure out where the shot could have

51

been fired from." Leaving Martika in the shelter of the cliff, Nancy walked toward the water.

"Nancy, don't!" Martika called out anxiously. "What if the person's still up there?"

"I don't think a sniper would stay around once we ducked out of view," Nancy replied, gazing up toward the top of the cliff. "In fact, he or she must have run off after taking the first shot."

"Why do you say that?" Martika asked.

"Because we kept standing out there for a minute before we realized what had happened," Nancy reasoned. "A shooter could have gotten off a second shot easily."

Scanning the railing above, Nancy caught sight of the gazebo overlooking the far end of the beach. "There," she said. "That gazebo would have been the perfect spot. Come on, let's go check it out," she said, heading for the far set of steps. "Martika, does anyone know you take walks down here at night?"

"Everyone on the staff," Martika said, following Nancy. "They have to know where to find me if I'm needed."

"That includes Kurt and Derek," Nancy pointed out. "And I suppose Christina could have found out, too."

After climbing the steps to the top of the cliff, they entered the gazebo, which was empty. Nancy shone her flashlight beam along the ground. It didn't take her long to find what she was searching for. "I was right," she said, picking something up and showing it to Martika.

"What is it?" Martika asked.

"A shell," Nancy told her. "From a small pistol, I'd guess." Nancy pocketed the shell and peeked back down at the beach. The view was unobstructed, and the full moon shone brightly. The shot would have been relatively easy for anyone with experience in marksmanship. Martika had been extremely lucky. Nancy wondered if she'd be so lucky the next time.

Martika shuddered. "What do we do now, Nancy?"

"We go back inside," Nancy said, meeting her gaze squarely. "And you lock yourself in your suite until the police get here."

At that, something snapped in Martika. "Absolutely not. Nancy, I told you. If I call the police I'll be sabotaging Cloud Nine!" There was an hysterical edge to her voice.

Nancy touched her shoulder gently. Keeping her tone calm but serious, she said, "Whoever did this means business, Martika. I know you don't want to alarm your guests, but you can't risk your life, either."

"There's got to be another way," Martika insisted. "Earlier you suggested I get one of the security staff to be with me at all times. How about if we do that? I know I refused before, but it's a better alternative than calling in the police."

"It won't help against bullets," Nancy said, shaking her head.

"I know just the person for the job," Martika went on. "And I'll be careful, I promise, Nancy." The model hugged herself. "I've just got to keep things calm. Everything's riding on it. Please try to understand."

"All right," Nancy said at last, knowing that there was little she could do in the face of Martika's resistance. "But I want you to lock yourself in your suite for the night."

"I will, definitely," Martika said with a wan smile. "I guess I am feeling a little shaky." She laughed nervously and squeezed Nancy's hand. "I feel as though you saved my life," she whispered, her eyes filling with tears.

"Come on," Nancy said. "Let's get you back inside." She led Martika into her suite, searched it quickly, then said good night and headed up to her room.

Bess and George were already asleep, though they'd left the light on in the bathroom for Nancy to see by. She suddenly felt exhausted—it had been a long day. She got ready for bed quickly, knowing that she'd need to be rested and alert the next day. While everyone else at Cloud Nine relaxed, she'd be on the job.

When Nancy woke up the next morning, the light was streaming in through the windows. Bess and George's beds were empty, though she found a note on the bureau telling her to meet them at breakfast.

She showered and dressed in under fifteen minutes, putting her bathing suit on under her shorts and tank top. Then she headed down to the patio, where breakfast was being served. She spotted her friends at a table shaded by a pink-and white-striped umbrella. They had plates of fresh fruit and muffins in front of them and were filling out their program cards.

"Bess, all these workouts—step class, yoga, high- and low-impact aerobics!" Nancy said, once she'd taken a seat. "Are you sure this is a good idea?"

Bess rolled her eyes. "I'm not a wimp. I can handle it."

Nancy grinned. "Whatever you say." Turning to George, she asked, "What about you? What have you got planned?"

"I have tennis with Kurt, a shiatsu massage, a run on the par course, and maybe water aerobics." George's eyes twinkled. "I can't wait," she said. "What a fantastic day! How about you, Nan?"

Nancy told her friends what had happened on the beach the night before. "So I'm not going to fill out a program card. I'm just going to wander around and talk to people."

"Let me know if you need any help," George offered.

"I will," Nancy replied. "We'll talk again at lunch. For now I just want to scout things out."

Soon after, the girls went their separate ways. Nancy's first stop was the mineral baths outside the beauty center, where she found Christina Adams soaking herself in a steaming pool shaped like a large U, entertaining Helen MacArthur, Morgana Ricci, Sadie Thomas, and Mrs. Smythe with gossip about Martika. Nancy took off her shorts and top, grabbed a fluffy white towel, and got into the pool with them. "Ahhh," she said as she adjusted to the steaming, sulfurous water. "This is relaxing."

"Isn't it?" Christina agreed. "Everyone, this is Nancy Drew. I met her last night at dinner. She says she's here as a guest—but I happen to know she's a detective."

Everyone in the pool turned to Nancy with renewed interest. The *Savoir Faire* editor's face was covered with a cosmetic mask, but Nancy could tell that she was particularly intrigued.

"Who told you that?" Nancy asked casually.

"Oh," Christina said airily, "a little bird on the staff." She laughed, then began to wheedle. "Come on, Nancy, tell us. What are you really here for?"

Nancy smiled tensely. "I do some detective work back home in River Heights," she said.

"But I'm at Cloud Nine for the same reason everyone else is."

"Christina, where are your manners?" Morgana Ricci asked. "Can't you see the girl doesn't want to talk about it?" The heiress splashed a little water on her face. "Just go on with what you were saying before she got here."

"Well," Christina said, "I understand Martika refused to put a penny of her own money into this place," Christina said. "It's all Preston Winchell's. That Martika's a pretty smart cookie. Smarter than I thought, anyway. Never lose your own money, I always say."

Everyone laughed except Nancy and Helen MacArthur. The editor listened carefully, though, and Nancy guessed that she was making mental notes. If Christina kept bad-mouthing Martika around Helen, it might result in some negative press for Cloud Nine.

"I also understand that Martika nearly had to put off the opening because Preston Winchell was so upset about cost overruns," Christina went on.

"Christina, dear," said Sadie Thomas, with a wicked grin, "how do you dig up such juicy dirt?"

"I never dig," Christina returned, waving a diamond-ringed hand. "I just keep my ears open, and I hear things."

Nancy couldn't help shaking her head. Christina Adams may or may not be the person behind all the incidents, Nancy thought, but she is certainly doing her best to spoil the opening of Cloud Nine.

"You know," Nancy said, breaking into the conversation. "I wanted to ask you about your own health spas, Christina. I looked for you last night around ten but couldn't find you."

"Oh, we were all in Morgana's suite, weren't we, Morgana?" Christina asked.

"Yes," Morgana said. "We've been inseparable since Christina got here. Isn't that right, Helen?"

"Except for when Christina went to her room to get the brochure for her new spa in Mexico," the editor said idly. She turned to Christina. "Remember, dear? I'm so glad you found it, even if it did take a little while. The Cozumel site appears to be glorious."

Nancy's ears perked up. "How long would you say you were gone?" she asked Christina.

"My, my," the spa queen replied. "You're certainly sounding very detectivelike. Why do you want to know where I was last night?"

Nancy lifted her hair off her shoulders. "Oh, I just wondered. I knocked at your door around ten, but there was no answer," she lied.

"Well," Christina said, reddening, "you must have just missed me. At any rate, what was it you wanted to ask me?"

"Oh, lots of things," Nancy said. "But they'll wait. Right now, I've got to find Derek. Have any of you seen him?"

No one had. "By the way," Nancy said as she got out of the pool, toweled off, and slipped her tank top over her head, "was Kurt Yeager with you all yesterday after Christina arrived?"

"For about five minutes or so," Helen MacArthur said. She looked at Nancy sharply. "Nancy, what's going on? You *are* doing some investigating. I can tell."

"No, not really," Nancy protested. "I was searching for him, too." She smiled cryptically, said goodbye, and strolled out of the mineral bath area. She'd gotten the information she needed, but now Helen MacArthur and Christina clearly suspected she was investigating. Nancy would have to be more discreet from now on.

Nancy wandered past the tennis courts, where she saw Kurt playing with a guest. She found Derek in one of the massage rooms at the beauty center. A woman was kneading the muscles in his shoulders.

"Hello, there," Derek said when Nancy poked her head around the doorway. "Come on in! Ooooh, right there," he instructed the masseuse, as she found a tight spot in his neck.

"Working hard this morning, I see," Nancy commented as she sat down in a nearby chair.

"Always," Derek replied dryly. "Nancy, right? You're the one who's friends with Bess. Did she tell you we're going dancing tonight?"

"She did," Nancy said, giving him a knowing smile. "In fact," she went on, ad-libbing, "we went looking for you last night, around ten. We couldn't find you."

"That's too bad," Derek said. "Did you check the dance club? I'm there every evening. I like to think of it as my little domain. Right, Sheila?"

The masseuse nodded and continued working on Derek. "I love to dance," she explained with a little smile.

"Too bad you and Bess didn't find us. There's no such thing as too much beauty in this world," Derek said.

Nancy had to keep herself from rolling her eyes. "But we did try the dance club," she fibbed. "Are you sure you were there the *whole evening?*"

"You did leave for a while, remember?" Sheila reminded Derek. "You said you had to talk to Martika. You were gone a long time. I remember I wondered what happened to you."

"Oh, yes. That's right," Derek said. "Thanks for reminding me, Sheila." He acted anything but grateful.

"I also wanted to ask you about the key to Martika's suite," Nancy went on. "She said you have one. Somebody got in there yesterday afternoon and fooled with her boa's cage."

"Really?" Derek asked. "That's pretty funny. To tell you the truth, I did misplace my key yesterday. I could have sworn I had it on my desk, but then when I checked it was gone."

Nancy remembered that Derek had had to pick the lock of Martika's suite when he went in to get the check, so maybe he was telling the truth about the key. "Well, see you later," Nancy said, getting up to go. "Don't work too hard."

"I won't," Derek called after her.

So, Nancy thought as she went back outside. Suspect number two had no better alibi than suspect number one.

Nancy took the long way back to the main building, around the tennis courts. She chose a path that ran near the drop-off to the shore, then turned toward the herb garden. The place was deserted, just as it had been the day before.

She paused for a minute by the entryway. Just then she heard a rustling behind her. Before she could swing around, she felt a powerful arm circle her neck from behind!

A hand covered her mouth, and Nancy was dragged backward into the garden. As hard as she kicked and twisted, she was unable to break free.

Then an angry voice whispered in her ear, "All right, Miss Detective. Suppose you tell me exactly what's going on."

Chapter
Seven

THE ARMS TWIRLED her around and then let go of her. Nancy found herself staring into the fierce eyes of Kurt Yeager. Taking a deep breath and facing him squarely, Nancy said, "You have a real knack for approaching people. Has anyone ever told you that?"

"Sorry," he said, his gaze down as he ran both hands through his blond hair. "But I have to know what's going on." Kurt sat down on one of the stone benches. "There's a rumor going around about you. If you're really a friend of Martika's, why haven't I ever heard about you?" He slapped his hands down on the bench, frustrated. "I know Martika doesn't trust me, but I'm doing the best I can in an awkward situation. I just can't figure out why she's hired a detective to keep an eye on me."

Nancy studied Kurt carefully. A moment earlier he had appeared so threatening, and now he was acting almost meek. "Okay, I'll level with you," she said. "But you'll have to level with me first."

"All right," Kurt said, nodding once. "What do you want to know?"

"First of all, why did you lie to me about why you were late for your body-sculpting demonstration?" Nancy asked.

Kurt bit his lip. "I-I'm sorry," he said. "I sort of took a little walk by myself. Sadie Thomas—the actress—said something pretty cruel about my performance in *The Flame Throwers*. I got mad and took off because I didn't want to blow up and take it out on one of the guests."

"I see," Nancy said. It was a plausible explanation, at least. "And where were you last night at around ten?" she asked.

Kurt frowned. "Why do you want to know?" he demanded. "Has something happened?"

"Uh-uh," Nancy cautioned, holding up her index finger. "I'm asking the questions first, remember?"

Kurt blew out a breath of air. "Okay," he said. "I was alone in the weight room. I don't get much chance to work out during the day, and I needed to blow off some steam."

"You resent Martika, don't you?" Nancy said.

"Wouldn't you if you were me?" Kurt asked. "She only hired me so she could humiliate me."

"Why did you take the job if that's the way you feel?" Nancy searched his eyes for any hint of evasiveness, but Kurt looked directly back at her.

"I *need* it," he admitted. "I lived pretty high after the Olympics, what with all the money from my commercial endorsements. But after my movie career flopped, nobody wanted me. I lost the house I'd built in L.A., my fancy cars—everything. You get used to living well, you know? I figure this is my chance to build up my bank account so I can strike out on my own again—set up a sports clinic, something like that."

"You'd like to see this place fail, though, wouldn't you?" Nancy pressed on.

Kurt frowned and stared at the ground. "Well," he said softly, "I'd love to see Martika eat a little humble pie. But on the other hand, I do need this job. Besides, believe it or not, I still care about Martika. In spite of everything." He met Nancy's gaze levelly. "Does that answer your questions?"

"Just one more thing," Nancy said, sitting down next to him. "You're not a very good speller, are you?"

Kurt laughed. "Everyone knows that," he said. "I'm dyslexic. Hey, no one's good at everything."

Nancy laughed lightly.

"Now it's my turn," he said. "Why are you spying on me?"

Nancy decided to take a chance and be honest with him. "I'm here to protect Cloud Nine, actually," she said. "And Martika. Someone took a shot at her last night."

Kurt sprang up from the bench and spun around to face Nancy. "What are you talking about? Who did it?"

"If I knew that, I could relax and go swimming," Nancy said calmly. "I thought it might be you."

"Me?" Kurt started pacing back and forth. "Are you nuts?" Then he stopped and faced her again. "Oh, I get it. I've got a motive, right? Well, so does Christina Adams. So do lots of people. Martika has a real talent for making enemies."

"Martika got three threatening notes," Nancy told him. "All with misspellings in them."

"I see," Kurt said slowly. "So someone's trying to make me seem guilty. Now I understand." He paused and after a moment continued. "Do you think I sent them?"

"I can't rule you out," Nancy said. "But I'd appreciate your help from now on. It would help clear you of suspicion."

"Anything I can do," he said, offering her his hand. "And sorry about grabbing you. I had no business doing that." Smiling at her as he got up, he said, "I've got to go. Good luck, Nancy. I hope you get to the bottom of this soon." Kurt took off, leaving Nancy alone in the herb garden.

Well, she thought to herself. Kurt Yeager had just been surprisingly frank with her. Or had he? His sincerity could have been an act—a way to gain Nancy's confidence so he could stay one step ahead of her investigation.

She got up slowly and after a while made her way to the patio behind the main building. About an hour later, George and Bess joined her, and they decided to have lunch as she filled them in on her morning.

"Wow!" George said when she heard about Nancy's encounter with Kurt. "No wonder he was so quiet when we played tennis."

"Well, I just can't believe he'd try to kill Martika," Bess said with certainty. "He's got honest eyes. People with honest eyes are never killers."

Nancy resisted the urge to mention all the criminals with honest eyes she had helped put behind bars. "How was your workout, Bess?" she asked, changing the subject.

"Total torture," Bess said, rolling her eyes. "And I didn't lose a single pound—I weighed myself afterward."

"Go easy on the tartar sauce," George warned

her cousin, pointing to the broiled tuna sandwich on her cousin's plate. "Working out isn't going to do you any good if you slather that stuff on your food."

"But it tastes so much better," Bess moaned. She pushed her plate away and stood up. "I'm out of here, anyway. I've got another torture session in ten minutes—low-impact aerobics this time." With a dramatic groan, Bess stood up and went off to her next appointment.

"I've never seen Bess this disciplined about exercise," George said.

"It *is* amazing," Nancy agreed. "I guess it's something about being at a spa."

Nancy rose from the table, too. "George," she began, "you said you might want to do some snorkeling. Are you up for it now?"

"Sure," George replied, "but I thought you'd be checking out suspects, not tropical fish."

"Actually," Nancy said, "I'd like to snorkel out to Christina Adams's yacht. It may not be as much fun as looking at coral, but it could be a lot more educational."

"Count me in. I'll skip the par course," George said with a mischievous grin. "Let's get ready."

Half an hour later Nancy and George were down at the scuba shack near the wharf. There they were fitted out with snorkeling gear. "Just walk down this little beach to the end and wade in," the staffer at the shack told them. "It's a short swim out to the reef."

The surf was gentler than it was behind the main house, although the sandy beach was much narrower. Nancy and George walked to the very end of it, where the rocks jutted seaward and the underwater trail began.

Donning their gear, Nancy and George swam out beyond the rocks and the trail, heading toward the opening in the reef that surrounded the island. Christina's yacht was anchored just outside the reef, in open water near the western end of the island.

The yacht was enormous—at least seventy feet long. Christina Adams could afford it, though, Nancy thought. After swimming up to the stern of the boat with George beside her, Nancy grabbed onto the bottom rung of a steel ladder on the port side.

Nancy pulled back her mask so she could examine the exhaust holes of the ship. "If there were engine problems, you'd think they'd have gotten a mechanic from Saint Thomas by now," she said. "Let's go on board and have a peek."

"Do you think it's safe?" George asked.

"It seems deserted to me," Nancy said.

With that, they climbed quietly on board, took off their flippers, and held them. They found the companionway stairs, and started down.

They had passed through the main cabin and galley when they heard voices farther down the hall. "That must be the crew, working on the engine," Nancy whispered. "Let's listen." George nodded silently.

"What was it supposed to be, Cap'n?" a man asked. "Engine trouble?"

"That's what the boss lady said, Charlie," a second man answered. "In fact, we'd better spike her good before somebody comes out here to check. Should've done it last night. Got a monkey wrench handy?"

"Sure do, Captain," Charlie said.

"Good. Let's see, we'll just crack something that we've got a spare for. That way we can repair it quick when the time comes."

Nancy glanced at George, who was staring back at her. The captain and his mate were about to damage the engine on purpose!

"Go up and see if we've got any more of these," the captain ordered.

"Aye, sir," said the other man.

"We've got to get out of here, now!" Nancy whispered, pushing George back up the companionway and then following her.

They weren't fast enough. Just as Nancy reached the top step, she felt a hand grab her ankle and heard a man's voice below her.

"Hey, Captain!" he shouted. "Come see what I found!"

Chapter

Eight

NANCY GLANCED OVER and saw George already pulling on her flippers. "Jump!" Nancy yelled to her friend. At the same moment, before the man below her got a better grip, she grabbed the railing with her hands and twisting, kicked him hard in the stomach with her free leg.

The man grunted, let go of Nancy, and fell down the steps, crashing right into the captain, who had just appeared at the foot of the companionway. Nancy seized that moment to escape and stepped onto the deck. With her flippers still in her hand, she ran and vaulted over the railing.

She hit the water hard but held on to her flippers. As soon as she had air in her lungs again, she tugged them on, and then took off after George, who was far ahead of her.

To her relief, Nancy saw that the men did not

dive in after her. Nor did they get into the little motorboat to come after them. They would probably tell Christina about the incident, though, Nancy guessed.

Peering ahead, Nancy saw that George had missed the opening in the reef and was drifting far to the west, probably searching for another access point. Nancy took off, swimming hard after her.

She passed a buoy with a sign saying, No Swimming Beyond This Point—Dangerous Currents. George had snorkeled right by it!

Doubling her speed, Nancy felt herself being caught up in the current. She couldn't see George anymore, though she kept stroking hard against the water. She tried to stay close to the reef, where the current was a little weaker, hoping that George had done the same.

Soon Nancy found another break in the reef. She swam through it before she was pulled past, and found herself facing a jagged cliff.

She spotted a rock that jutted out of the sea in front the cliff. Nancy headed for the large black boulder and circled around it. There, to her relief, she found George, sitting on a ledge in the rock about three feet above the water.

"Are you all right?" Nancy panted, hanging on to the rock. "You missed the opening, and those currents were bad."

"I know. I'm fine, though," George said. "Nan,

did you see that?" She pointed to the cliff behind Nancy.

Nancy turned. Directly behind the rock was an opening in the cliff about fifteen feet wide and ten feet high. She hadn't noticed it before because the boulder had hidden it. Thick iron bars like those in a prison cell covered the opening, and behind them Nancy could make out a grotto.

"Let's check it out, George. Are you up for it," she asked.

"Absolutely," George replied, and dove smoothly into the water. It took them just a few minutes to cover the distance between the boulder and the grotto. They grabbed the iron bars and peered into the cave.

A pool of water covered the floor of the grotto, where a sleek speedboat was moored. The walls of the cave rose sharply around it. On the back wall, barely visible in the dark, was a little ledge just above the water line. A door covering an opening in the grotto wall rose above it.

"Wow!" George exclaimed. "What do you make of that, Nan?"

"I don't know," Nancy said. "But I bet we can find out from Martika." The gate was locked, so the girls had no alternative but to swim back toward the beach near the scuba shack, where they turned in their gear and then headed up the hill to the main building.

By the time they got back to their suite, it was late afternoon. They found Bess lying on her bed.

"Hey, Bess," George said. "You'll never guess what we found."

"I don't care," Bess groaned. "I'm exhausted."

"Tough day, huh?" Nancy asked, unable to suppress a grin. "Maybe you'd better skip dancing tonight."

"Are you kidding?" Bess countered. "What good is all the pain I've gone through today if I can't look great on the dance floor afterward? Besides, I lost only one pound. I've still got four to go. Maybe the rest will come off while I'm dancing."

"You know, Bess, maybe you'd better settle for just a week of fun in the Caribbean," George suggested. "You may be overdoing it."

Bess closed her eyes and inhaled deeply. "I'm making progress," she insisted. "No pain, no gain, they always say."

"You've got to work up to the kind of exercise you're doing or you might hurt yourself," George said firmly.

Bess dragged herself up to a sitting position. "I *am* already feeling sore. But I'm going to be as thin as Martika Sawyer if it kills me—which it probably will. Anyway, I'm taking tomorrow off from the torture. Check out my schedule card— seaweed wrap, mud bath, manicure—"

"Hey, it's almost dinnertime," Nancy said, checking her watch. "Come on, Bess. You should eat, even if it's just a little, to keep up your strength."

"Oh, twist my arm," Bess said, managing a grin. "Just promise me you won't let me eat dessert, no matter how hard I beg."

Nancy and George laughed as they all changed for dinner. While they got ready, Nancy and George told Bess about their afternoon adventure.

"Sure sounds like Christina Adams is guilty," Bess said. "The way she connived to get herself onto the island—"

"Yes," Nancy agreed. "But she's not the only one who looks guilty."

"You mean Kurt, right?" Bess said. "I already told you I think he's innocent because of his eyes, but let's see what you have against him. He can't spell, and he did know about the snake. Plus, he does have a temper, and he has no alibi for yesterday afternoon or last night when the shot was fired at Martika. Guess honest eyes aren't enough."

"That's all true of Derek, too." George reminded her cousin that the guy she was going dancing with wasn't above suspicion either. "And remember, he's definitely stealing from his sister."

"Gee," Bess said ruefully. "Why do the guys

we like always end up as suspects? They do look pretty guilty, though, don't they?"

"I'm afraid so," Nancy agreed, as they headed down to dinner. "Kurt resents Martika in a big way. Then again, Christina has the strongest motive to sabotage Cloud Nine. But Derek's a suspect, too. If his sister dies, he's her closest living relative. That means he'd probably inherit everything."

"Wow!" Bess said. "That's right."

"I'll have to check into that with Martika, of course," Nancy said, lowering her voice as they entered the dining room.

Martika was presiding over the crowd of guests, who were mingling before the food was served, chattering about their first day of workouts and beauty treatments.

Everyone seemed to be enthusiastic, Nancy noted—even Mrs. Smythe. She was all smiles as she told Preston Winchell about her personal beauty session with Martika. Kurt was doing his best to make the guests happy—especially the women.

Nancy went over to Martika and waited her turn to speak to her privately. "I thought you were going to get someone to keep watch over you," Nancy whispered.

"I already have," Martika replied. "But I don't need anybody when I'm in a crowd like this."

Nancy frowned but had to admit that Martika was probably right.

"How are things going?" Martika asked. "Have you found out anything more?"

"Plenty," Nancy told her. "When can we talk?"

Martika bit her lip. "Tonight's tough. Tomorrow morning? I can spare an hour or so after breakfast. We could go scuba diving together. Do you know how to dive?"

"Yes, but can't we talk sooner?" Nancy asked.

"I'm afraid not. Sorry." Martika gave Nancy's arm a squeeze. "But you're doing a terrific job, Nancy. Things are going great! Mrs. Smythe hasn't said anything about Squeeze, thank goodness. And Helen MacArthur told me she's very impressed so far. Oh, Nancy, I'm so happy—of course I'm scared, too. I'm afraid it might all come crashing down on me at any moment. Especially with Christina around. She still hasn't gotten her yacht repaired, you know."

"That's one of the things I want to talk to you about," Nancy said with some urgency.

"Right," Martika replied, brushing her off. "Well, I'd better go mingle. See you at the scuba shack at nine-thirty?"

"Okay," Nancy said. After Martika left, Nancy went over to say hello to Preston Winchell. "Hi," she said, introducing herself. "My name is Nancy Drew. I'm one of Martika's guests."

"Nancy Drew? Pleased to meet you," Winchell said, shaking her hand. "Have you met Mrs. Smythe?"

"Er, yes," Nancy said, as the elderly lady turned toward her.

Mrs. Smythe giggled. "We're old friends," she said, giving Nancy a little wink.

"I love your new haircut," Nancy commented.

"Oh, do you?" Mrs. Smythe said, overjoyed. "That Martika is a genius. My hairdresser at home would never have thought of anything as simple as this."

"I was just wondering, Mr. Winchell," Nancy said, changing the subject, "as Martika's partner, do you think things are going as well as I do?"

"Why, yes!" he said happily. "Trouble free, as far as I can tell. This week should put Cloud Nine on the map, provided everything keeps going so beautifully."

"Do you think there might be more Martika Sawyer resorts in the future?" Nancy probed.

"That all depends," he said cryptically. "If Cloud Nine does well, who knows? But if it doesn't, there are always other ways to invest one's money."

Nancy wanted to ask him what he meant by that, but just then Christina Adams floated over and gave Winchell a kiss on the cheek. "Preston, darling! Haven't they fed you yet? It's taking so long to serve dinner! Come on, you're wanted at my table." She held out her hand to him.

"Wanted? Who wants me?" he asked, with a mischievous glint in his eyes.

"I do," Christina replied, taking his hand and leading him away. "Pardon us," she said to Nancy and Mrs. Smythe.

"Isn't she beautiful?" Mrs. Smythe asked, gazing at Christina.

"She's one of a kind," Nancy replied.

That night the dance club rang with the music of a Caribbean steel band. The beat of the drums was irresistible, and everyone crowded onto the floor.

Bess had to stop after only two dances. Derek helped her back to her chair next to Nancy's. "Sorry, Derek," Bess told him. "I'm a little tired, I guess."

"Pity," Derek said. "How about you, Nancy? Would you like to stand in for your friend?"

"No thanks, Derek," Nancy told him. "I'm kind of tired myself. But don't worry, I know you won't have any trouble finding a partner."

Derek smiled as he started off. "I'm sure I won't," he added arrogantly.

"I'm devastated," Bess moaned. "Why did I work out so hard? Now I'm missing all the fun!"

"Poor Bess," Nancy said sympathetically.

"Maybe you'll feel better tomorrow night. Hey, we're here for a whole week, remember?"

"I guess you're right," Bess said, sighing. "I'm going back to the suite. Want to come?"

"No, thanks," Nancy said. "I want to stick around in case something interesting happens." Her attention was caught by George and Kurt, who were dancing up a storm. Martika was dancing with Preston Winchell—until Christina cut in and took him away. Nancy thought an argument might break out after that, but Martika contained her rage, and the night remained peaceful.

By the time Nancy and George were back in the suite and ready for bed it was after midnight. "Well, things seem to be going all right," George commented.

"It's too quiet," Nancy said. "Criminals don't usually stop until they get what they want. And this criminal hasn't yet got what he or she wants."

"Well, get some sleep, Nancy," George advised.

"Right," Nancy said, plumping up her pillow and falling back onto it. In moments she was sound asleep.

The next morning after breakfast, Bess went off to steam in the mineral baths, while George left for a lesson with Paul Flores, the tennis pro.

Nancy headed down to the scuba shack, where Martika was waiting for her in a shocking-pink diving suit. She was trailed by a female security guard. "See, Nancy?" Martika said, indicating the guard. "I did just what you told me to. Nadine is a tae kwon do expert, aren't you, Nadine?"

The pretty young woman nodded.

"Nadine, you can take some time off now," Martika suggested. "I'll meet you back in my suite at, say, eleven."

"Okay," Nadine said, shrugging. She turned and started back up the stairs.

Nancy collected her scuba gear and assured the instructor she was an accredited diver before going outside to slip it on. As she did, Martika asked, "What have you found out so far?"

"Well, for one thing, neither Christina, Kurt, nor Derek has an alibi for the night when the shot was fired," Nancy said.

"Ha!" Martika cried, helping Nancy with her air tank. "But which one do you think did it? You don't suspect Derek, do you?"

"I don't know what I think yet," Nancy said. "But this will interest you. Yesterday afternoon George and I found out that Christina's boat doesn't have engine trouble at all. In fact, she told her crew to cripple the engine, in case anyone from the island came out to check on it."

"I knew it had to be something like that,"

Martika said, her eyes blazing. "Of course, it's too late now to throw her off the island. What I'd really like to do is throw her off the cliff!"

"Speaking of cliffs," Nancy said as they began a systematic check of their scuba gear, "when George and I were swimming back from Christina's yacht, we found a grotto with a locked gate and a boat inside. What's it for?"

Martika seemed taken aback for a moment, but then she replied, "Oh, that. It's in case of emergency. You can get to that little boat without going outdoors. There's a tunnel leading down from the main house, cut right through the rock."

"I see," Nancy said.

"Anything else we need to discuss before we go diving?" Martika asked.

"Just one thing. Do you have a will?"

"Well, that's a creepy question." Martika's ice blue eyes appeared troubled for a moment, but then they danced mischievously. "Yes, I do, as a matter of fact. And to answer your next question, Derek inherits everything. Anything else?"

"Not right now," Nancy said.

Martika nodded. "Wait till you see what's under here," she said, wading into the clear aquamarine water. A few other divers were headed out to the reef, but Nancy lost sight of them when she dove and began swimming seaward.

The day before, when she and George had gone

snorkeling, Nancy had been too preoccupied with Christina's yacht to notice much. Now, in the space of a minute or so, she saw an eel, some clown fish, a school of manta rays, and a lumbering sea turtle. Enchanted, she followed the turtle until it disappeared on the far side of the reef. She turned back and saw Martika, gesturing for her to go on.

The reef was a true wonderland, and Nancy took her time to explore it. She tracked the sea turtle for a while, then, realizing how long she'd been separated from Martika, scanned the area for her. Finally she caught sight of the model's hot-pink diving suit on the other side of the reef.

Something was wrong.

Martika was flailing her arms and legs wildly, clearly panicking.

Nancy swam closer. It wasn't until she actually reached Martika that she could tell what was happening. Her heart leapt to her throat at the sight.

Martika's oxygen regulator was in her mouth, and the other end of the tube was attached to the oxygen tank, but the two ends were no longer connected.

Martika's oxygen line had been cut in half!

Chapter

Nine

MARTIKA WAS STRUGGLING so violently that Nancy had a hard time helping her, but then all at once she seemed to collapse. She must be passing out, Nancy realized.

Nancy grabbed her as she began to sink, knowing that Martika would be dead in a matter of minutes if she didn't act quickly. Taking a deep breath, Nancy removed the regulator from her mouth and pushed it into Martika's. Breathe! she thought. Breathe, Martika!

Martika's eyes opened as she sucked in the life-restoring air, but Nancy could tell her hold on consciousness was tenuous.

Nancy slipped Martika's left arm around her shoulders. Placing her right arm around Martika's waist, Nancy kicked hard for the surface, struggling to make it before she had to take her regulator back. She was afraid Martika would really panic if she had to remove the regulator from her mouth. Nancy was dizzy and seeing a wash of red across her field of vision from lack of oxygen as the two of them finally broke the surface near a head of coral.

Nancy tread water as she sucked in lungfuls of air. She was grateful they hadn't been deep and could surface quickly. After a minute she guided Martika to the head of coral, where they lay to recover. It was a long time before Nancy's heartbeat returned to normal.

"Oh, Nancy!" Martika sobbed. "I thought I was dead!"

"What do you think happened?" Nancy asked, studying Martika's oxygen line. It was apparent that it had been cut neatly in two.

"I felt something tug on my line," Martika said. "At first, I thought it was you. The next thing I knew, my line had been cut. I panicked. Nancy, you saved my life! How can I ever thank you?"

"Let's not worry about that now," Nancy said quickly. "This line has definitely been severed. You're sure you didn't notice anyone nearby?"

"I don't think so, but I wasn't really looking," Martika said, distress pinching her voice. "There were several divers around on our way out to the reef. But I lost track of them almost as soon as I dove in."

Nancy nodded. She hadn't paid any attention to the handful of other divers she had seen either. "Well, we'd better get back to the island," Nancy said. "Do they keep a list of who takes out equipment at the scuba shack?"

"No," Martika said. "We're on the honor system here once we've checked you out as a qualified diver. Whoever was handing out equipment today might remember who came by if he wasn't too busy. But some guests prefer to use their own equipment, so he wouldn't see everyone anyway."

The two of them swam for shore and handed in their gear. Nancy saw Derek running toward them from the dock. "There you are, Martika!" he shouted as he approached. "I've been looking everywhere for you."

"Well, now you've found me," Martika said curtly.

"Do you know what time it is?" Derek asked his sister. "It's after eleven."

"So?" Martika asked. Nancy knew he wouldn't know about Martika's telling Nadine she'd see her at eleven.

"Have you forgotten about Maura McDaniel's make-over?" he asked her. "You were supposed to meet her at ten-thirty to supervise it."

"Maura McDaniel . . ." Martika repeated distractedly. "Oh, yes, our contest winner—the plain Jane from Australia. I'd totally forgotten about her."

"New Zealand," Derek corrected her. "She's from New Zealand, and she's waiting for you at the beauty center."

"Oh, all right, I'll go," Martika said impatiently. "Tell her to wait a minute. I've got to go back to my suite and change first." Turning to Nancy, she added, "Wait till you see this girl when I get through with her!" With a wicked smile and a wave of her hand, Martika started up the long flight of steps to the main building.

"She's amazing," Nancy said out loud, watching as Martika climbed the steps. Not only had Martika recovered physically from her brush with death, but she also seemed to have shaken free from the shock. She's a very resilient young woman, Nancy thought.

"*Amazing* is the word, all right," Derek agreed, getting into a golf cart. "Well, I'd better go tell Cinderella that her fairy godmother is on the way."

"Just a minute," Nancy said. "How long were you looking for Martika just now?"

"I don't know," Derek said, perplexed. "Half an hour or so. Why?"

"Just wondering." Nancy looked hard at him. He was dressed in a Hawaiian shirt, shorts, and beach thongs. It would have been possible for him to have cut Martika's oxygen line and changed clothes someplace down here. "Did you see or speak to anyone while you were searching for Martika?"

"Lots of people," Derek countered.

"And how long ago did you see Maura McDaniel?" Nancy pressed.

"Fifteen minutes ago, I guess." Derek acted annoyed now. "What's this all about, anyway?" he demanded.

"Oh, nothing," Nancy said, brushing him off. "I'm just curious about a lot of things around here—like the Cloud Nine corporate checkbook."

Derek went white. "I don't know what you're talking about, but whatever it is, you'd better stay out of other people's business. Curiosity killed the cat, remember."

"I'll remember that," Nancy said with a little nod. "In case somebody around here winds up dead."

Derek stared at her. "Don't think I'm not onto you, Nancy Drew."

"What do you mean?" she asked, narrowing her eyes.

"When I saw your name on Martika's personal guest list it surprised me because I didn't recognize it. So I did a little research, made a few calls, and found out what you do. You're a detective."

Nancy nodded in acknowledgment. "That's right," she said. "I am. I thought Christina had told everyone by now. I guess the two of you don't speak."

"No, we don't, but now that I know, I think I know why she asked you here. It was to spy on me, wasn't it? Sweet of her." With that, he guided his cart back up the hill.

Nancy gazed after him. She wondered whether she'd done the right thing by scaring him a little. If Derek were behind the murder attempts, her scaring him might be just what was needed to get him to stop. On the other hand, it might make him that much more dangerous.

Back at her suite, Nancy found an invitation on the coffee table, asking her and her friends to dine with Martika that night at a dinner for her special guests. Sounds like fun, Nancy thought as she pocketed the invitation to show Bess and George.

Lunch was served on the patio again—an enormous buffet featuring seafood salads and tropical fruit. Bess was in line with George, trying to decide what to eat. "My calorie count says to stay below twelve hundred a day," Bess complained, "but it's impossible! I'd have to eat nothing but lettuce and kiwifruit!"

"I can think of worse fates," Nancy said. "How are your aching muscles?"

"Much better," Bess said. "I hit the whirlpool and the sauna, and then I had a Swedish massage you wouldn't believe. After lunch I'm getting a seaweed wrap. If I can't lose weight, at least I'm going to *look* fantastic."

Nancy showed Bess and George the invitation to Martika's private dinner. "All right!" Bess said happily. "Are you going to sit with Kurt, George?"

"I'll sit wherever they put me," George shot back. "Bess thinks I'm in love with Kurt."

"Are you?" Nancy asked.

"Of course not," George retorted. "Just because he said I have gorgeous eyes—"

"When did he say that?" Nancy asked.

"At tennis this morning. He came by while I was getting my lesson," George replied.

"To comment on your form," Bess said, giggling.

"He asked me to watch the fireworks with him tonight," George said. "They're going to shoot some off from the edge of the cliff." Putting her plate down on the table, she added, "Hey, Nan, there's a step class at two-thirty. Want to come?"

Nancy peered across the patio to where Martika was standing with Nadine right behind her. Seeing Nancy, Martika waved and pointed to Nadine, as if to say, "See? I'm well protected."

"I guess so," Nancy said. "Things seem pretty quiet—for the moment."

After lunch Bess went to the beauty center, and Nancy and George headed for class.

At the workout center several different classes were going on at once. Nancy and George watched one called Abs, Tushes, and Thighs for a few minutes, then went into the locker room, where they changed into exercise clothes and stowed their bags.

They entered the studio just as the instructor began fiddling with the tape player in front. The girls got their step units and prepared for the workout of their lives. Nancy had never tried stepping before, and she really liked it. By the time a quarter hour had gone by, she was into the rhythm of it.

When the class was over, she and George decided to spend what remained of the afternoon by the pool. They ordered sodas and lay in lounge chairs at the deep end, where one of the fitness staffers was wowing a small crowd with one fancy dive after another.

It was near five when the girls began collecting their things. By the time they got back to their suite, Bess was there, getting ready for Martika's special dinner.

Soon the girls were dressed in the best outfits they'd brought. Nancy thought Bess was fabulous in a peach-colored dress that dipped off her shoulders and had a full skirt. She'd set it off with a single strand of freshwater pearls.

George's classic cream-colored silk tunic over a slender black crepe skirt was fantastic, too, especially when she twisted a black and gold braided belt around her waist.

Nancy had chosen a sky blue dress with spaghetti straps. She'd pulled her burnished reddish blond hair into a high ponytail.

Bess grabbed a silk flower from an arrangement in the bedroom and twisted it around the band that held Nancy's hair. The effect was perfect.

"Well, I think we look great!" George exclaimed. "Put us on the cover of *Savoir Faire!*"

"And guess what, you guys," Bess said excitedly, "I weighed myself again, and I lost another half a pound—without even working out! Isn't that super?"

"Super," Nancy repeated, with a broad smile.

The girls made their way downstairs to a glass-enclosed garden room at the far end of the building. The staff had set up tables there for the night. There were flowers at every place setting, and the silverware glistened in the soft light. In the far corner of the room was a large gold cage containing a brightly colored cockatoo.

Most of the two dozen guests were already there. Nancy and the girls watched for Martika but didn't see her.

A maitre d' entered and asked that all the guests be seated. Nancy took a quick inventory of those present: Kurt, Derek, Helen MacArthur, Mrs. Smythe, Morgana Ricci, Preston Winchell —the whole group from the yacht trip over except for Maura McDaniel. Christina Adams hadn't been invited, of course.

Finally Martika made her entrance, to a polite round of applause. She was radiant, as usual— but Nancy thought there was something different about her.

As Martika took her seat and greeted her guests, a murmur began to spread throughout the room. "That's not Martika!" someone said out loud. Nancy saw that it was true. It wasn't Martika at all. It was—

Chapter

Ten

M AURA MCDANIEL!" Nancy gasped.

The wallflower from New Zealand had been transformed into a dazzling, dark-haired beauty. Her makeup was perfect, and her hair had been attractively cut and styled. It was almost as if Martika had created a sister for herself.

Now Martika herself entered the room in a dress very much like Maura's and threw her arms around the girl, who stood to greet her. The guests applauded, clearly thrilled by Martika's little ruse. The glowing Maura sat down beside Martika, and the model signaled to the waiters for punch to be served.

"What an incredible job!" George whispered in Nancy's ear. "I can't believe that's the same girl we met on the boat."

"It's her all right," Bess said. "I'm going to

try to schedule a make-over with Martika myself."

On Nancy's right, Helen MacArthur said to Preston Winchell, "I've got to get a photo spread of this. What a sensation it'll make!"

Nancy smiled as the waiters went from table to table, placing individual goblets of fuchsia-colored punch in front of each guest. Then Martika rose to speak.

"I'd just like to say thank you to all my special friends," she began. "Cloud Nine has been my dream for a long time, and now it's coming true. I'm just so happy that you're here to be a part of it." She flung her arms open wide. "And I hope I'll be able to say the same thing a year from now, when I open my next resort."

This remark was greeted with more applause. Raising her punch glass, Martika toasted her guests.

"By the way," Martika continued, "after dinner tonight there'll be a fireworks display over the beach. I hope you'll all attend. So, without further ado, let's drink to the continued success of Cloud Nine, and to more perfect health for every one of us."

Everyone joined her. A buzz of conversation rose up from the group, which Martika hushed. "I've got another toast to make," she announced. "This one's to the man whose generous financing made all this possible. Preston Winchell!"

Winchell got up to acknowledge the applause with a broad, contented smile.

"And I'd also like to thank—" Martika began.

Derek rose from beside her just then. Putting his arm around his sister, he said teasingly, "Enough toasts. Can't we eat dinner? I'm starving." He turned to the guests and grinned. "She was always a talker—even when we were kids."

Martika put her hands on her hips in mock anger but let Derek plop her down in her seat, laughing. She leaned over and kissed Maura on the cheek.

Dinner went without a hitch, and Nancy felt a sense of relief when Nadine entered and escorted Martika from the room. Secure in the knowledge that the bodyguard would keep an eye on Martika, Nancy headed up to her suite to get a sweater, and then went back outside to the patio for the fireworks.

The area was so full of people that Nancy had trouble finding anyone she knew. The night was hazy, and a stiff, cool breeze was blowing.

Nancy saw Preston Winchell talking with Maura McDaniel and went over to them. "Hello, Maura," she said. "Congratulations. I guess everyone's been telling you how fabulous you look."

Maura blushed, and Preston Winchell answered for her. "I was just telling her that myself."

At that moment Christina Adams appeared at Winchell's side and slipped her arm through his. "Preston, darling," she cooed, nuzzling up to him. "I've been looking for you everywhere! Come with me—I want to introduce you to some friends of mine." Before Winchell could object, she dragged him away, leaving Maura and Nancy behind.

"What an operator!" Nancy said, shaking her head.

"I think she's horrid," Maura said. "The way she gossips about this place, and after Martika let her stay here when her boat broke down."

"Well, I don't think she'll change Preston Winchell's mind about supporting Martika," Nancy said reassuringly. "He seems pretty thrilled with the way things are going."

"So am I," Maura said happily. "Do you really like my new look?"

"It's fantastic," Nancy said sincerely.

"You don't think I look too much like her?" Maura asked nervously.

"You mean Martika?" Nancy said. "Well, no, not really. There is a resemblance, but I notice she did your hair a little differently, and the eye makeup is less severe." In truth, Nancy was reaching for differences. In the dark and at a distance, anyone could mistake the New Zealander for Martika.

"You won't believe how many people have noticed me tonight," Maura said with a happy giggle. "Oh, Nancy, I feel like my life is just beginning."

"I'm thrilled for you, Maura. You deserve to be happy," Nancy replied.

"Thank you," Maura said quietly. "You know, my father left me a lot of money when he died. My lawyer keeps telling me I should make a will, but it seemed so futile. I've got no one to leave anything to. Now that I'm beautiful, though, maybe I'll get married someday."

"Maybe you will," Nancy told her.

"It's just that I've always been so shy," the young woman went on.

"Maura!" The two of them turned around and saw Martika approaching, followed by Nadine. "There you are, dear," she said. "Aren't you cold in that off-the-shoulder dress? Here, take my wrap." Martika lifted the gold lamé shawl off her own shoulders and tucked it around Maura.

"Oh, no, I couldn't, Martika—what'll you wear?" Maura asked.

"Don't worry about me," Martika said. "I'm flushed with excitement. Everything's going so well. Anyway, I have to get the fireworks started," Martika added, hurrying away. "Enjoy, you two!" She beckoned to Nadine, who followed closely behind her.

"I'm going to the ladies' room to check my makeup," Maura said after that. "Want to join me?"

Nancy shook her head. She watched as Maura disappeared through the glass doors that led back into the lobby. Then she turned around. Bess and Derek were standing by the railing not far from her. She went over to them.

As Nancy approached, Derek caught a glimpse of her. He whispered something in Bess's ear and quickly walked away. Soon he had melted into the crowd.

"What did he say to you just now?" Nancy wanted to know.

"Oh, he was just whispering sweet nothings in my ear," Bess said with a giggle. "Really, Nan, you don't have to worry. Derek hasn't got a murderous bone in his body. Although, I must say, he is awfully curious about you. He keeps asking me all these questions about what you're doing and what you're thinking."

"Uh-huh." Nancy nodded knowingly. "Be careful around that guy. He's definitely one of our chief suspects."

"Okay, Nan," Bess said. "But I'm telling you. You're wrong about him."

Just then the fireworks began with a big blast. Seconds later, thousands of tiny pink and white lights spilled out of the sky above the cliff. Three staff members were setting off the fireworks at the edge of the cliff. One starburst after another exploded overhead. The display was elaborate, and it lasted for almost forty-five minutes. Nancy was beginning to get tired of craning her neck to look up. She lowered her head and peered down at the water but couldn't make out much.

When the display finally ended, the crowd broke up. Nancy saw Nadine heading toward the lobby—without Martika!

Quickly Nancy searched for the model but didn't see her. She could feel panic rising inside her until she finally spotted Martika standing at the head of the stairs near the gazebo.

Noticing Nancy, Martika beckoned to her. Nancy walked over to Martika and said, "Why did you send Nadine away?"

"Oh, come now," Martika protested as she started down the stairs. "Can't I even have a private walk on the beach?"

"No," Nancy answered. "You can't. Don't you realize what kind of danger you're in? Someone's already tried to kill you twice in the last forty-eight hours. How bad does it have to get before you take it seriously?"

"I take it seriously," Martika said. "But you're here with me. You'll come along, won't you?"

"Of course," Nancy replied, beginning to descend the steps. When they reached the first landing, they stood quietly for a while, looking out. Nancy began to relax a little. Maybe her presence and that of the bodyguard had scared off the would-be murderer.

The breeze was stiff, and Martika shivered in the cold. "Wait here for me," she told Nancy. "I'll be right back. I'm just going up to get a wrap."

Before Nancy could protest, Martika was running back up the few steps they'd come down. It was just about this time two nights before that someone had taken a shot at Martika, Nancy realized. But a few minutes later, when Martika returned wearing a soft gray shawl, Nancy felt relieved.

The two of them started down again, Nancy in front. About two-thirds of the way a loud bang rang out from below them. They both jumped in surprise and took off running the rest of the way down to the beach.

At first glance the long strip of sand appeared to be deserted.

"What do you think that noise was?" Martika asked. "It sounded like a shot."

"Maybe it was just a leftover firecracker," Nancy said as they walked out onto the beach.

Then Nancy saw something lying on the sand,

about twenty paces away. She ran toward it, her dread increasing with every step.

A person lay with fixed eyes staring at the stars, a glittering gold lamé shawl spread like a halo surrounding her head. Nancy froze when she saw the woman's face—it was Martika Sawyer.

Chapter

Eleven

Nancy knew it couldn't be Martika, of course. It had to be Maura McDaniel. Nancy bent down to check her vital signs. Maura was dead, and somebody had killed the wrong person.

Gingerly Nancy lifted the woman's shoulder and saw that a bullet had struck Maura in the back. The bullet hole was small—about the size of the one in Martika's sleeve. It had left no exit wound in Maura's chest, so the New Zealander looked as if she were resting.

"Horrible!" Martika gasped, staring at her look-alike's dead features. "Oh, Nancy, I can't believe it!" Tears trickled down Martika's beautiful face, and she bit down on her fist to keep from sobbing out loud.

Nancy fished a tiny flashlight from her purse to check for clues. At first she saw nothing—no telltale footprints in the powdery sand, no weapon.

Then Nancy spotted something in Maura's hand. She bent down and saw that it was a shred of paper. She removed it and held it up to the beam of her flashlight.

"What is it?" Martika asked.

"A small piece of newspaper," Nancy informed her. "There's a little bit of printing on it. It says *The Auckland Gazette,* November fifteenth. Auckland is in New Zealand, where Maura was from," Nancy added more to herself than to Martika. She pocketed the shred of newsprint.

"Not much to go on," she said. "Still, it's all we have. Maybe the police can find more. And, Martika, we *are* going to call the police."

"Right." Martika nodded. "I understand. Oh, Nancy, why didn't I listen to you yesterday? If I had, this poor girl might be alive now."

"You had no way of knowing this would happen," Nancy said, consoling her. "You thought you were taking a gamble with your own life, not with anybody else's. Anyway, bringing the police in might not have saved her."

"I suppose not," Martika agreed. "Well, let's go up and call them."

"You go ahead," Nancy said. "I'm going to stay here and make sure nobody disturbs the body. Just be careful, Martika. Remember—the killer may have already realized his or her mistake."

"All right," Martika said.

"If you run into anybody who seems surprised to see you, make a note of it, okay?" Nancy instructed.

"Yes," Martika replied soberly. With a last shuddering glance at the corpse, she ran for the steps.

Alone with the body, Nancy tried to reconstruct the murder. Maura had been shot in the back but had fallen backward from the impact. It appeared as if the killer hadn't gotten a good enough look at her to know she wasn't Martika. Maura had been wearing Martika's gold lamé shawl, after all.

Nancy wondered about the piece of newspaper in Maura's hand. If the killer had examined the body after the shooting, he or she would have discovered it and in frustration might have ripped it from the dead woman's hand. But why take the paper? Was there something important in that particular newspaper? It was two months old, after all.

Nancy paced down the beach a little way toward the steps she and Martika had come down. She saw something on the sand there and trained her flashlight on it. She bent down to pick it up. A spent firework. Funny, Nancy thought, pocketing it. This wasn't anywhere near where the fireworks had been set off. Also the wind hadn't been blowing hard enough to carry it off.

Nancy was with the body when the police helicopter flew in and landed on the beach. Several officers scrambled out and ran to the corpse. They roped off the area, setting up floodlights and photographing the crime scene. While a forensics expert examined the body, other officers combed the beach for clues.

The commotion soon drew a crowd of onlookers. Guests and staff alike gathered around to see what was happening. Reporters and photographers were there, too, of course. They stood just outside the ropes, yelling out questions and taking photos.

Nancy saw Martika behind them, watching the proceedings with anxious eyes. No doubt she was visualizing the devastating headlines that would soon be screaming off the front pages of tabloids everywhere.

Nancy spotted Bess and George in the crowd. Kurt and Derek were there, too.

Christina Adams was standing near Nancy in a tight knot of onlookers. "This is absolutely awful!" she was saying. "But, really, who would want to kill a poor, pathetic child like her?"

Who indeed? Nancy wondered. No one at the resort had anything against Maura McDaniel, as far as she knew. There were many people who might want to kill Martika Sawyer, though— including Christina Adams herself.

As the body was loaded into the helicopter, an officer stepped forward, his white uniform contrasting with his rich brown skin.

"Ladies and gentlemen!" he called out to the crowd. "I am police Captain Steven Logan from Charlotte Amalie, Saint Thomas. As you all know, there has been a homicide here tonight. You can rest assured we will soon find out who is responsible. Until we do, however, we need your help."

A murmur ran through the crowd, but Logan persisted. "I must ask you all to remain at Rainbow Cay until further notice. Indeed, I request that you go to your rooms and stay there until we call you in for questioning. For now I would like to see the persons who found the body."

"Captain Logan?" Nancy called out as she and Martika approached him. "Ms. Sawyer and I discovered the body. My name is Nancy Drew."

"Ah," the captain said, giving her a nod before turning to Martika. "Ms. Sawyer, how do you do? I have seen your face many times, of course, but it's a great pleasure to meet you."

"Thanks," Martika said coolly.

"I'd like to speak with you one at a time," the captain said. "Ms. Sawyer, you first, if you don't mind."

"Of course," Martika said, nodding.

"Captain," Nancy interrupted. "While you're talking to Martika, there's something up in my suite I'd like to show you. Do you mind if I go to get it?"

"Go ahead," he said. "But hurry back. We have many people to question, and I want to get as much as possible done tonight."

"Right." Nancy dashed up the steps to the main house. There she found the premises being searched by at least a dozen officers. They must have come by boat while we were down at the beach, Nancy realized.

In her suite Nancy found George and Bess sitting in the living room, talking about the murder. "Oh, Nan, isn't it awful?" George said. "Poor Maura!"

"Really," Nancy said sadly as she retrieved the spent shell she'd found in the gazebo. She felt in the pocket of her sweater. The popped firework and the piece of newspaper were still there. "Just as she was feeling positive about starting a fabulous new life." Nancy felt the anger rising inside her. "Whoever killed Maura isn't going to get away with it. Not if I can help it."

"At least the police are involved now," Bess said.

"True," Nancy agreed. Going over to her friends, she said, "George, do you know where Kurt was during and just after the fireworks?"

"No," George answered. "When the fireworks started, he said he had to go do some stuff. He didn't say what. I didn't see him after that."

"What about you, Bess?" Nancy asked. "Can you account for Derek's whereabouts?"

"Sorry," Bess said. "He took off during the fireworks, too."

"Interesting," Nancy said. "And there are a lot of other loose ends—like what was Maura doing down on the beach in the first place, and why did she have a two-month-old newspaper in her hand? If a silencer was used when someone shot at Martika, why wasn't one used tonight?"

"Gee, Nan," Bess said, biting her lip. "It is pretty confusing."

"It sure is," Nancy agreed. "Well, I'd better go see Captain Logan. He's probably wondering what's keeping me."

As Nancy went down the stairs to the lobby, she encountered an officer on his way up. "Ms. Nancy Drew?" he addressed her.

"That's me," Nancy replied.

"Captain Logan sent me to tell you he is

interviewing suspects in Ms. Sawyer's suite. Will you please accompany me?"

"Suspects?" Nancy repeated. "Am I a suspect?"

"Everyone is a suspect at the moment," the man replied.

When they got to Martika's suite, Nancy saw Logan sitting at the desk, making notes. Martika was nowhere in sight.

"Ah, Ms. Drew," he said, smiling at her. "Sit down, please," he added, indicating the chair beside the desk.

Nancy sat, and as soon as she did, Logan rose and started pacing. "Ms. Sawyer has informed me that she asked you here as a private detective," he began. "Is that correct?"

"Yes," Nancy said.

"You have been here for three days and have witnessed several troubling incidents, I am told. Yet you never contacted the police, is that correct?"

Nancy swallowed hard. "Yes. I'm afraid that's true," she had to admit.

"According to Ms. Sawyer, you were present when a snake was set loose, Ms. Sawyer's oxygen line was cut, a bullet went through the sleeve of her blouse—and when Maura McDaniel was found dead on the beach."

"Well," Nancy said finally, after it became clear that he was waiting for her to explain herself, "I'm impressed. You've done a very good job of finding things out, Captain Logan."

The captain smiled wryly.

"Of course, you're right, Captain," Nancy continued. "I should have insisted that Martika call in the police."

The captain seemed to relax a bit, but he was still suspicious. "Now, why don't you tell me what you've found out through your own investigations?"

"All right," Nancy said. "I've brought a few things to show you."

Captain Logan drew up a chair next to hers as she emptied her pockets and explained each of the items she had brought. By the time Nancy was through, Captain Logan had become much more respectful of her. "I wasn't implying that you are the killer, mind you," he assured her. "I was just doing my job."

Nancy nodded. She could tell that he didn't consider her a suspect anymore. Now maybe they could work together to solve the case.

Just as she was about to say so, however, the door of the suite burst open, and an officer entered, panting. In his hand, wrapped in a white handkerchief, was a small pistol.

"Captain!" the man cried. "We found the murder weapon!"

"Twenty-two caliber," Logan said, inspecting

it. Nancy noticed that the automatic pistol was small, lightweight, and black. No shiny surfaces to reflect and bounce light on a moonlit night. No silencer.

"Where did you find it?" Logan asked.

"In Kurt Yeager's suite, sir," came the answer. "Right under his pillow!"

Chapter

Twelve

Nancy rose from her chair in surprise. "Under his pillow?" she repeated.

Before she could say anything else, Captain Logan cut in. "Have you arrested the suspect?" he asked his man.

"Yes, sir, but not without a struggle. He's a very strong man, and he gave Sergeant Curtis a bloody nose. At any rate, we've got him now."

"Has he confessed?" Logan asked.

"Not yet, sir," the officer responded. "He keeps insisting he's innocent."

"All right, Jenkins," Captain Logan said, taking the gun from him. "Take the suspect back to headquarters in Charlotte Amalie. I'll interview him myself."

"Yes, sir," Jenkins replied. Saluting Logan, he hurried from the suite to carry out his orders.

Logan turned and smiled at Nancy. "Well, Ms. Drew," he said, turning the pistol over in the handkerchief, "it looks as if we've solved this case in record time."

"How can you be so sure?" Nancy asked him. "Don't you think that if Kurt were guilty he would have gotten rid of the pistol before you searched his room? He had plenty of time to ditch the gun. Why didn't he?"

"Ms. Drew," the captain said, his smile vanishing, "at this point I must ask you to leave the rest of the investigation to us. As you said yourself, you should have called us sooner. One person is already dead. I am not inclined to leave a killer at large just because there is a slight chance he is not guilty. At any rate, perhaps we will find his fingerprints on the murder weapon."

"But, Captain—" Nancy began.

"Ms. Drew!" Logan interrupted. "Please return to your suite now. I will have you sent for if I need anything further from you. Oh, and thank you for these," he added, indicating the clues she'd given him.

He opened the door for her, then spoke to a man standing guard outside. "No one is to leave the island until we have a signed confession. And keep an eye on Ms. Drew, here. I don't want her making any more trouble."

Nancy was speechless. She could tell that no matter what she said, Captain Logan was not going to listen. Without another word, she marched out of Martika's suite. By the time she got to her room, she was steaming. She slammed the door behind her as hard as she could.

"Nan?" came George's voice from the bedroom. "Is that you?" Seconds later George and Bess entered the living room in their nightgowns.

"Sorry, guys," Nancy said. "I didn't mean to make so much noise, but I was angry."

"What's up, Nan?" George asked.

Nancy quickly told them about Kurt's arrest. George was aghast. "He's innocent!" she said. "Can't they see that?"

"But what about the gun, George?" Bess reminded her cousin, putting an arm around her shoulders. "If they found it under his pillow . . ."

"It could have been planted, Bess," Nancy cautioned. "I'm not so sure he's guilty. Kurt may not be a genius, but if he killed Maura, I don't think he'd be dumb enough to put the murder weapon under his pillow where the police could easily find it."

"I guess you're right," Bess agreed.

"Why didn't the killer just toss the gun in the water, anyway? It probably would never have been found," Nancy continued. "It seems to me that someone is trying to implicate Kurt."

"Nan," Bess said, "you don't think it was Derek, do you?"

"I don't know what to think," Nancy admitted. Checking her watch, she said, "It's one-thirty in the morning. I'm exhausted. Let's get some sleep. There'll be time to sort things out in the morning."

The next morning, as Nancy and her friends were getting ready for breakfast, there was a knock on the door of their suite. Opening it, Nancy was surprised to see both Martika and Derek.

"May we come in?" Martika asked.

"Of course," Nancy said, leading them to the sofa, where they sat down. George and Bess came into the living room, too, and sat in the wicker armchairs. Nancy could tell that both Martika and Derek were upset, even though Martika was showing it more.

"Oh, Nancy," Martika said. "It's horrible, just horrible! I told the police captain that it couldn't be Kurt, but he wouldn't listen." Martika buried her face in her hands. Derek put an arm around her to comfort her, but she shook him off coldly.

"Martika," Nancy said sympathetically, "this has hit you pretty hard, I know."

"I still love him, Nancy," Martika said, raising her tear-stained face. "I don't know why it all went wrong, but I still feel for him, deep down. That's why I gave him the job here. I hoped that once he got himself together . . ." Martika couldn't go on. She started to sob.

"If it makes you feel any better," Nancy said, "I don't think Kurt is the murderer either. I think someone set him up." She explained to Martika and Derek what she had told Bess and George the night before. "And another thing," she added. "There was no silencer on the gun."

Martika had stopped crying now. She and Derek stared at Nancy. Bess and George seemed confused, too.

"What do you mean, Nan?" Bess asked. "Maybe the killer just threw the silencer in the ocean and kept the gun to make Kurt look guilty."

"Possibly," Nancy replied. "But why not just put the gun and silencer under his pillow?"

"What if there wasn't a silencer?" George asked.

"Then why didn't I hear a gunshot the night Martika was shot at on the beach?" Nancy pointed out.

Out of the corner of her eye, Nancy saw Derek flinch. He glanced at Martika for a second and then collected himself.

He had just given something away, Nancy knew. He'd realized something—but what was it?

"Maybe the killer used a silencer for his first attempt but didn't bother with it last night," Bess suggested.

"Or what about that spent firework you found,

Nan?" George asked. "Maybe it was what made the sound of the shot."

Again Nancy saw the light go on and off in Derek's eyes. "Er, excuse me," he said, getting up and checking his watch. "This is all fascinating, but I have to get to work. The guests need my attention."

Martika got up to join him, but Derek said, "You stay here, Martika. You'll feel better if you let yourself talk things out with Nancy. I'll take care of everything." Before Martika could protest, he was out the door.

That wasn't like Derek, Nancy reflected. He was acting so diligent and helpful. Something was wrong with the picture. If only she knew what.

Martika became restless and uncomfortable once Derek had gone. "You know," she said, rising abruptly, "I really should get down to breakfast myself. The guests will be gathering, and I ought to take charge before the gossip gets out of hand. Christina will be there, you see— and so will Preston. She's sure to try to convince him to pull his money out of my spa, what with the murder and all. And the newspeople. Who knows what they're writing about all this? I'd better get down there right away!"

Having worked herself up into a nervous state, Martika hurried out of the suite. When she was gone, George said, "What just happened, Nan? Why did they both get so nervous and leave so abruptly?"

"I don't know," Nancy said, going over to the door. "But I'm curious to find out. Why don't we go down to breakfast and see? I want to keep an eye on Christina Adams, too. As far as I'm concerned, she and Derek are both still suspects. I'd be interested to know how she's reacting to Kurt's arrest."

Breakfast was served in the dining room that morning. All the guests were talking in hushed tones about the events of the night before. Martika was standing by the buffet table, conversing somberly with several guests. To Nancy's surprise, Derek wasn't there. Nor were Christina Adams and Preston Winchell.

The girls helped themselves to the buffet and then found a table. Before Nancy started eating she scanned the room again. This time she couldn't find Martika.

"Something is up," Nancy told Bess and George. "Now Martika's disappeared." She rose quickly. "Let's split up to cover more ground. We're searching for Martika, Derek, Christina, and Preston."

Bess went outside to search, George headed for Martika's suite, and Nancy went back to the lobby. As she approached the registration desk she asked the clerk, "What's the number of

Derek Sawyer's suite? Martika asked me to send for him."

"We can't give out that information," the man said. "But I'll send someone with your message."

"Thank you," Nancy replied. She found a seat in the lobby and picked up a magazine from a table, pretending to read as she watched the clerk give the message to a bellhop. When the bellhop strode out of the lobby, Nancy followed him.

The uniformed man went up the stairs and down to the end of the corridor. Nancy hid at the top of the stairs as the message was delivered.

She waited for the bellhop to pass her on his way back down the stairs. Then she went down the corridor, and stopped in front of Derek's suite. Putting her ear to the door, she heard the muffled sound of Derek's voice.

"Just realized . . . truth . . ." Nancy could make out only a word here and there, but what she heard confirmed her suspicions. Derek *had* figured out something important that morning.

"Know what you've done . . ." Nancy held her breath, pressing her ear even harder against the door, praying that nobody would walk down the corridor and find her.

Derek must have taken a few steps toward the door, because now she could hear almost every word he said. "You know I can prove it," he said. From the long pause that followed, Nancy guessed that he was talking to someone on the phone. Could it be the person he'd promised more money to?

"I found the old newspaper article from New Zealand in your room, and I've got it," Derek said menacingly. Nancy had to stifle the urge to gasp. This was not just someone Derek owed money to—this had to be the person who had killed Maura McDaniel!

Chapter

Thirteen

DEREK'S NEXT WORDS told Nancy everything she needed to know.

"So let's not have any more fuss about money, shall we?" he said. She could hear the sneer in his voice. "From now on we're equal partners."

Equal partners! Was Derek blackmailing someone? Who would he want to become equal partners with? His sister, Martika? That didn't make any sense, Nancy thought. Sure, he'd want to be partners with her, but Martika had been the killer's intended victim—three times!

That left only one possibility. Derek had to be talking to Christina Adams.

Nancy was now desperate to get inside Derek's suite. She wanted to see the newspaper article he'd mentioned.

She raced back down the hall to the lobby.

George and Bess were just coming in—Bess through a rear door and George through the front. "I went to Martika's suite," George said. "No one answered."

"I've searched the grounds," Bess added wearily. "No sign of anyone."

"Listen," Nancy said. "I've got a plan, and I need your help."

Pulling them back into the corridor so no one could hear, Nancy quickly told her friends what she'd learned at Derek's door.

Bess was obviously relieved. "Nan!" she said. "That proves he's not the murderer, doesn't it?"

"I guess it does," Nancy had to admit. "But he's still dangerous, and now that he's trying to blackmail a murderer, he's in danger himself. Which is why you've got to be careful with him, Bess."

"What do you want me to do, Nan?" Bess asked.

"Get him to go someplace with you," Nancy replied. "Someplace where there are a lot of people around. I don't want you to be alone with him. I just need him out of his room for an hour or so."

"That might be easier at night," George said, "when the dance club is open."

"We can't wait that long," Nancy replied. "He's in his room now. You'd better get going,

Bess. After you're both out, I'll search his suite. Derek said he could prove whoever he was talking to was the murderer. So let's hope he wasn't bluffing. George, I want you to call police headquarters on Saint Thomas and ask to speak to Kurt. Find out exactly what he did after he left you last night. It may give us a clue. Then meet me in Derek's suite." Nancy grabbed her friends' hands. "Good luck, guys. And, Bess, be careful."

Bess ran up the stairs while George went off to make her phone call. Nancy followed Bess as far as the top of the stairs, waiting in the same spot where she'd watched the bellhop deliver her phony message to Derek. From there she could see Bess outside Derek's door. Soon it opened and Bess went in.

Then Nancy waited—and waited. Through the window on the landing below her, she saw Christina walking arm in arm with Preston Winchell outside. She couldn't hear what they were saying, but Nancy knew well enough what Christina wanted from him. Now that there had been a murder at Cloud Nine, maybe she had already lured him and his money away from Martika.

"Come on, Bess!" Nancy said under her breath. Ten minutes had gone by, and still she remained inside Derek's suite.

Finally Bess and Derek emerged, Derek with a

tennis racket in his hand. Stopping to make sure his door was locked, he led Bess down the hall toward Nancy.

Nancy fled down the stairs and ducked into the ladies' room off the lobby. After a couple of minutes, when she felt sure that Bess and Derek had gone, she headed back up the stairs.

Using the lock pick she carried in her handbag, Nancy wasted no time in getting Derek's door open.

She stepped inside, and her heart sank. Derek's suite was an incredible mess, with papers scattered everywhere.

Nancy realized she'd never have time to sort through them all. Imagining his looking at the article as he threatened the killer, she went straight to the desk, where the phone was, to begin her search.

One stack of papers caught her eye—photocopies of financial projections for the resort. They didn't belong there. Martika would never have involved her brother in the resort's finances. What was more, the copies appeared to have been made in a rush, with the printing off center or even running off the page. It made Nancy wonder whether Derek had made the copies in a hurry and on the sly.

The projections were hard to decipher, but Nancy was able to understand two things from them. First, most of the money that had built

Cloud Nine came from one source—Preston Winchell. Second, the resort was on shaky financial ground. Not nearly enough money had been put into it to keep it going for more than a few months. That meant that unless there was a large new infusion of money, the resort probably would not survive.

Just then there was a knock on the door. Nancy jumped right out of Derek's chair, her heart pounding. Thankfully, it was only George.

"Captain Logan wouldn't let Kurt talk to me," George said with a frown.

"Never mind," Nancy told her. "Help me sort through all this stuff."

"What are we looking for?" George asked.

"A newspaper article from New Zealand," Nancy explained.

George sat down in a chair facing the opposite side of the desk and began going through the piles. Nancy's gaze fell on one of the papers George discarded.

"George, this is a handwritten letter from Preston Winchell to Martika!" she said excitedly. "And it's dated this morning. Winchell must have given it to Martika himself. How did Derek get hold of it so fast?"

"Maybe when he left our suite, he went straight to his sister's," George suggested. "Martika was with us for a good five minutes after he left, remember? And then she went down to the dining room and was there without him, for at least a little while."

"Right!" Nancy agreed. "She was fidgety after he left. She must have suspected he was up to something. So she made a quick appearance at breakfast and then started tracking him down."

"What does the letter say?" George asked.

"It says that in light of the fact that a murder has been committed at Cloud Nine, he is no longer willing to provide sole financial backing to keep the resort going. He's demanding that Martika provide matching funds from her own reserves. He reminds her that he asked her to do so before the resort opened. She said she couldn't swing it, so he went along. Apparently, he's not willing to now."

"Sounds like Cloud Nine is in trouble," George said.

"Right," Nancy agreed. Checking her watch, she added, "Bess and Derek may be coming back pretty soon. We've got to find that newspaper article. Now, where could it be . . . ?"

Just then Nancy glanced up at a bookshelf across the room. A volume there was lying on its spine, with a piece of paper protruding from it. Nancy went over and took down the book. Opening it, she drew out a folded page from a newspaper. "I've got it, George!" Nancy cried triumphantly.

The page was slightly yellowed, but there was

no doubt it was the right one. The paper had been ripped across the upper right-hand corner, where the date and name of the newspaper had been. "Let's get out of here, George," Nancy said excitedly. "We'll read it outside."

Nancy led George out of the suite and down the hall toward the side exit nearest the tennis courts. Outside, they found a quiet spot near a hibiscus tree and read the article.

"'November fifteenth,'" Nancy began out loud. "'Peter McDaniel, of Auckland, was found dead in his home early this morning.' It's an obituary—for Maura's father!"

Nancy read on. "'The sixty-five-year-old millionaire died of natural causes. He is survived by his only child, Maura, twenty-seven, who will inherit his entire estate."

"Whew," George said. "That would have made Maura pretty rich."

Nancy kept on reading. "'Mr. McDaniel, born Peter Sawin, had lived in Auckland since 1972, when he left the United States in disgrace after a brokerage scandal—'"

Nancy's jaw dropped. "Sawin!" She stared at George, who was staring right back at her.

"George," Nancy said softly. "Maura told me the night she died that she hadn't made a will since she had no family. She *did* have a family, though! She just didn't know about them. But one of them knew about her."

"I don't get it," George said, confused.

"This means," Nancy began, excitement flooding her voice, "that on Maura's death, her entire fortune goes to her nearest living relatives. And they are her cousins—Derek and Martika Sawyer!"

Chapter

Fourteen

NANCY AND GEORGE stood by the hibiscus tree a long moment before either spoke. On the exercise track ten feet away, guests were jogging by, utterly unaware of all that was going on.

Finally Nancy said, "This changes everything, George."

"I'll say," George agreed.

"After Maura was murdered, I passed Christina Adams talking to a bunch of people," Nancy said. "She was wondering why anyone would want to murder poor Maura. At the time, I thought the same thing. I thought the murderer had to have mistaken her for Martika Sawyer. But I was wrong!"

"Wait a minute, Nancy," George broke in. "Somebody's been trying to kill Martika, too. But who?"

"It could be Derek," Nancy said. "We know that he's a sponger and a thief."

"I guess it runs in the Sawin family," George said grimly. "Look at their uncle Peter."

"Good point," Nancy said, nodding. "So, suppose Derek learned that Maura McDaniel was his cousin and that she had no living relatives. Maybe he even found out that she hadn't made a will. He could have cooked up the contest, made sure Maura got an entry form, and fixed it so she won—meaning she had to come to Cloud Nine. He must have planned to kill her *and* Martika, so he'd end up with Maura's money and his sister's as well.

"If that's true, Derek Sawyer's a dangerous man," George said tensely.

"We've got to find Bess," Nancy said. "Come on, there isn't a moment to lose!"

Nancy took off down the path to the tennis courts, with George right behind her. When they got there, Bess and Derek were nowhere in sight. "Just what I was afraid of," Nancy said under her breath.

"What is it, Nan?" George asked.

"If they aren't playing tennis," Nancy replied, "they may not be where people can see them. Which means, we'd better find them *now.*"

"There's Paul Flores," George said. "Let's ask him if he's seen them."

Nancy and George ran over to the tennis

instructor. "Was Derek Sawyer here with a blond-haired girl?" Nancy asked him.

"They came by a little while ago," the instructor said. "But the courts were full. So I guess they decided to do something else."

"Where could they have gone?" Nancy said.

"The beach?" George suggested.

Nancy's eyes widened as she took off toward the cliff.

Near the railing Nancy spotted a gardener trimming a hedge. "Have you seen Derek Sawyer?" she asked him.

"Yes, he was with a young woman," the man told them. "They went down to the beach."

"Uh-oh," Nancy said.

The two girls dashed to the stairs. About halfway down they stopped on a landing to catch their breath.

George suddenly said, "There they are, Nan! Way down the beach!"

"Bess!" Nancy called out. "Beeessss!"

The wind was blowing against her, and the surf was crashing on the shore. Nancy knew there was no way Bess could hear. Derek had his arm around Bess's shoulder and almost seemed to be leading her away.

"Come on, George," Nancy told her friend. "We don't have a minute to lose!"

The two girls flew down the remaining steps. Once they reached the beach, the going was slower because their feet sank in the glistening sand.

"Beeess!" Nancy yelled again.

The couple had stopped beneath the cliff. Nancy could see her friend's blond hair whipping in the breeze.

"Beesss!" George screamed.

Now Bess heard them. She waved happily, while Derek stared, clearly not pleased. Nancy and George ran up to the couple.

"Hello there," Derek said with a tight smile.

"Nan! George!" Bess said, acting bewildered. "What's going on? Is something the matter?"

Nancy nodded, but she addressed her words to Derek. "I want the truth, and I want it now, Derek. There's no use lying—I overheard you on the phone saying that you had the newspaper article."

"I—I—" Derek stammered.

"Correct me if I'm wrong," Nancy cut in impatiently. "Somehow you found out that Maura was your cousin and that her father had left her a lot of money."

"No!" Derek cried, his frustration apparent.

"Yes," Nancy replied. "You decided to get your hands on it, so you cooked up the scheme to get Maura to come to the opening so you could kill her."

"Stop," he growled, his hands balled into fists.

"Why should I?" Nancy said harshly. "It's the truth, isn't it?"

"No, no, no." Suddenly he seemed ready to collapse, his head hanging to his chest. When he spoke again, it was in a breathy whisper. "You don't understand—"

"What?" Nancy asked tensely.

"It was Martika," he said, shaking his head. *Martika.* She killed Maura—not me. She lured her to Cloud Nine."

"Martika!" George gasped.

"But someone was trying to kill *her,*" Bess said, incredulous.

Derek stared straight at Nancy. "That's what she wanted you to think. It was amazing, the way she set it up to look like she was in danger."

Nancy stood rooted to the spot, her heart pounding hard, the details of the case flooding through her brain. The silenced shot on the beach, the severed oxygen line, Maura's make-over, and the gold lamé shawl, the spent firework Nancy had found, the loud bang Nancy had taken for gunfire, the newspaper article . . .

"What you're saying," she began slowly, "is that Martika planned to kill Maura, but to keep from being a suspect, she arranged it so she appeared to be the intended victim." Nancy took a long, ragged breath. "So I wasn't invited here to be Martika's investigator. I was invited here to be her alibi."

"You got it," Derek said, relieved that he'd made Nancy believe him. "But don't be too hard on yourself. My darling sister was incredibly clever."

"I don't understand," Bess said, perplexed.

"You see," Derek began, "just before our father died, he told us that his brother had fled to New Zealand after the scandal. I never thought much about it, but Martika was obsessed by it. She was old enough when the scandal happened to know what our family went through. She started reading newspaper clippings about it, going through New Zealand phone books trying to find Sawins. She didn't know Uncle Peter had changed his last name, too, which was only natural, of course."

He sighed for a moment before continuing. "She went off on a job in New Zealand last November. She read the obituary and knew Peter was our uncle and Maura our cousin. Next thing I knew, she told me she'd run a contest in New Zealand to pick a guest to come to our opening for free. All Martika told me was that this Maura person had won, and I was to write and tell her so. I never suspected till I found that article in Martika's room this morning. Then, of course, I figured it all out. I don't know why she kept the article."

"A kind of vanity," Nancy explained. "She assumed she'd never be caught."

"And what about the murder attempts?" Bess asked.

"All faked," Nancy said. "Each and every one of them. Starting with the notes. Easy enough to forge, misspellings and all. She must have mailed the first two from Saint Thomas and dropped the last one on the floor in her room so she could find it while I was there that first day. Martika had to pin Maura's murder on someone, and Kurt was the obvious choice. She acted upset when he was arrested, but she must have planted the gun under his pillow herself."

"And it would have been easy enough for her to let the snake out of its cage before she went down to the dock to greet us," Bess speculated.

"Right," Nancy said.

"What about the shot somebody took at Martika that first night?" George asked. "How could that have been faked?"

"She could have fired the gun through her blouse sleeve earlier," Nancy reasoned. "Then she probably dropped the shell in the gazebo before she invited me for a walk down on the beach. At just the right moment she raised her arms over her head, pretended to hear something whiz by, and waited for me to do the detecting work. I always assumed that because I heard no bang, the shooter was using a silencer. But there never was a silencer. There was no bang because there was no shot!"

"But what about the other murder attempt?" George asked.

"The diving accident? She could have hidden a knife under the sleeve of her wet suit and cut the line herself. She said she didn't see anyone in the water, and I believed her. Someone could have come up behind her without being noticed.

"And now comes the most brilliant part of Martika's scheme," Nancy continued. "When she had me convinced that someone was trying to kill her, she set the stage for Maura's murder."

"Because it was Maura she wanted dead all along," George half-whispered.

"She did a make-over on her cousin, so that Maura looked just like *her!* Then she lent her the gold lamé shawl. While the fireworks were going on, she must have invited Maura down to the beach. She showed Maura the obituary and told her who she really was. Maura must have turned and moved away from Martika while she was reading. All Martika had to do was wait for a big fireworks blast and shoot. When Martika grabbed the obituary back, she didn't notice the small piece that remained in Maura's hand."

Nancy watched Derek's face turn ashen. The whole plan was too much for him to take in.

"So after Martika killed Maura, she ran up the steps and planted the gun under Kurt's pillow. Right?" George asked.

"She had a master key," Derek said quietly.

"In fact, she was the one who probably took mine."

Nancy nodded. "Then she went back outside and invited me to go walking with her. But on the way down the steps, she pretended to feel cold and ran back up to get a wrap."

"I get it now," Bess exclaimed. "That's when she lit the firecracker and threw it down the cliff."

"Exactly," Nancy said. "I was already a little way down the stairs. Her timing was perfect. The firecracker must have had an extra long fuse—easy enough to arrange. Presto—an instant alibi for Martika. Hearing the bang, we ran down onto the beach and found Maura. The charade was complete. The police located the gun and arrested Kurt. Everything was perfect until Derek found the obituary and tried to blackmail her."

No one said anything for a long moment. At last Derek cleared his throat, though his voice remained hoarse with emotion. "It was strange. When we were in your room this morning, something just clicked. I had no idea how intricate Martika's plot was, but I suddenly knew she had to be behind everything."

"So you went to her room . . ." Nancy prompted him.

"Yes," he went on. "And found the article. I know I should have tried to stop her, but I decided to cash in on the situation by blackmailing her instead. Martika deserved it."

"And you needed the money," Nancy said. "Who were you talking to on the phone that first evening when you took Martika's check?"

"A man on Saint Thomas," Derek said. "I owe him some money. You see, I gamble quite a lot."

"Derek—" Nancy said, but suddenly she stopped. She could hear pebbles ricocheting down the cliff. One bounced off her shoulder, stinging her.

"Hey," Bess said, dodging a pebble. "What's going on?"

Raising her eyes to the cliff top, Nancy gasped in horror as a roar sounded.

"It's a rock slide!" Nancy cried. "Everybody run."

Just then, though, a large boulder started to move above them. It came loose with a grinding sound and then hurtled down the cliff, headed right for them. In another moment one of them would be crushed!

Chapter

Fifteen

LOOK OUT!" Nancy screamed, grabbing Bess and yanking her away. The two of them fell to the sand and rolled away just as the boulder hit the beach.

"George!" Nancy cried out as soon as the big rock landed.

"I'm okay, Nan," came George's voice from nearby. Nancy and Bess both heaved sighs of relief.

"Me, too," Derek said, "but let's get out of here before another one falls."

They all ran down the beach, pausing at the steps leading up to the gazebo.

"That was close!" George gasped.

"Too close," Nancy agreed, checking the spot where the slide had started. "I bet this was no accident. Come on, everyone. We've got to stop Martika before she does any more damage!"

Nancy led the group back up the steps at a breathless pace. They emerged at the top to find the patio mostly deserted. Nancy took off running toward the spot at the top of the cliff where the slide had started. It was well beyond the end of the railing. When she reached it, she saw a little path leading down to a perch in an outcropping of rocks. She followed it, gripping the boulders along the sides of the path with her hands.

When she came to a stop, she found herself at the very edge of the cliff. There, abandoned on a ledge, was a large wooden plank.

George was right behind her. "What is it?" she asked.

"I believe Martika's been here," Nancy said. "This must be what she used to start the rock slide. She could have jimmied a couple of rocks free and pushed them over."

George inhaled sharply.

"Let's go back up," Nancy said.

When they reached the top, Derek and Bess were waiting for them. "Obviously, Martika must know that we're onto her," Nancy told them. "That's why she tried to kill us just now. You're her brother, Derek. Where should we search for her?"

Derek shrugged. "She must have seen that we were still alive. If I were Martika, I'd be running for dear life at this point. And since this is an island, that means the dock."

"Right," Nancy agreed. The four of them ran back to the main building and through the lobby, exiting out the front door. They scanned the entire harbor area and saw no boats except for the ones moored to the dock.

"Let's check Martika's suite," Nancy said, swinging around almost without skipping a beat.

When they reached the model's room, Nancy was surprised to find the door open. She exchanged wary glances with her three companions before leading them into the suite.

The main room was empty. Nancy made a quick check of the bedroom and bathroom. Squeeze was sleeping in his cage, but Martika was gone. One thing was obvious—she had left in a hurry. Martika had seen that the game was up and had gone through her papers in a rush. She had probably destroyed anything that could possibly implicate her.

Nancy was about to suggest that they split up to search for Martika, when the bookshelf on the wall next to the desk caught her eye. There was something wrong with it. It seemed to have been moved away from the wall.

She went over to check and found that the bookshelf was slightly out of alignment.

Derek helped her push it away from the wall.

"It's a secret door!" Nancy gasped. It was

made of strong wood and had a heavy iron latch. She grabbed the latch's handle, pulled hard, and the door sprang open. "There are stairs going down!"

"They're cut right into the rock," Bess said.

"George—the grotto!" Nancy cried in sudden realization. "Martika said there were stairs cut into the rock leading down from the main house! Come on, everyone!" she shouted, bounding down the dimly lit steps. "We've got to stop her before she gets away!"

The stairs went on forever, and as she hurried down, Nancy realized that Martika had had an escape route from the very beginning.

Nancy could finally see the iron door at the bottom of the stairs. It had a push handle on it. Nancy rammed into it with her right side, forcing it open. Derek, Bess, and George were right behind her as she barreled through the doorway.

Then several things happened almost at once. The door slammed shut behind them with a colossal clang. Bess swung around to stop it, but she was too late, and though she tried to shove it back open, it wouldn't budge. It was locked. They couldn't get back up the same way they'd come.

Nancy had turned back to watch Bess as she struggled with the door. Now she faced the pool again. There, standing at the stern of the little speedboat, was Martika—flushed and incredibly beautiful, holding a large leather briefcase in her left hand and a semiautomatic pistol in her right. The pistol was leveled right at Nancy and her friends!

They were trapped. Martika had left the bookshelf awry on purpose, Nancy realized, to lure them down here. Now she could finish them off and no one would even hear the shots.

"Welcome," Martika said, with a satisfied smile. "Please put your hands above your heads."

The four of them did as they were told. Nancy looked around. She and her three companions were still standing on the small rock ledge at the rear of the grotto. Just in front of them, the ledge ended and the water began. The small boat fit neatly into the tiny mooring place. On the other side of it, the steel bars closed off the opening of the cave.

"You're really something, Nancy," she said, with an admiring nod of her head. "When I invited you here, I never thought it would come to this. I'm really sorry to have to kill you and your friends. As for you, Derek, it was only a matter of time. There was no way I was going to share Maura's fortune with you. You'd have squandered your half and been after mine in no time."

"Don't I have a wonderful sister?" Derek commented dryly.

"Shut up!" Martika ordered, jabbing the gun in his direction. Derek quickly complied.

"You've always been a loser, Derek," Martika said bitterly. "What were you ever good for except to gamble away my hard-earned money? When Dad died, did you lift a finger to take revenge on our uncle? No. You were only interested in one thing, and that was having a grand old time for yourself.

"Well, I went out and did something for our family," she went on. "I tracked down Uncle Peter and his only daughter. I lured her here so that I could take revenge for Dad. *I* did it all. Why should I have shared the reward with you?"

"You did it to save your business," Derek contradicted her. "You knew Winchell was going to pull out, and you needed to replace his money. And there was no way you were going to risk your own. No, that's all put away in a secret account on some safe Caribbean island where you can spend the rest of your life without a care in the world. Isn't that right?"

Martika's smile widened, and she raised her perfect eyebrows. "Why, Derek, you're smarter than I thought. But you're wrong about one thing. I did do it for revenge—most of all. The money was secondary. Of course, now I'll never get to see that money. Once they find your bodies, it will be only a matter of time before they put two and two together. Fortunately, I'll be long gone by then."

Nancy looked from sister to brother and back again. The hatred between them was almost tangible.

Martika raised the briefcase she was holding. "There's a bomb in here," she informed them. "It's a little present from me to you."

Then, blowing them a kiss, she pressed a button on the briefcase. "There," she said. "That ought to make things exciting in just a minute or two. I wish I could say it's been nice knowing you all."

Martika backed toward the steering wheel as she continued. "I'm sorry it had to end like this, but you have only yourself to blame, Nancy. If you hadn't done such a good job, things would have worked out better for all of us."

Martika was up against the wheel now. She reached behind her and pushed a remote control button on the console. Instantly the iron gate in front of the grotto opened, providing free passage for the boat.

As Martika turned around to rev up the engine and make her escape, Derek suddenly sprang into the boat, making it wobble wildly. He yanked his sister around, reaching up for the gun she held above her head. The two of them wrestled for a minute.

Then there was a shot.

Bess screamed, and she and George dropped to the ground for cover.

With a loud grunt of pain, Derek fell forward toward Martika.

Seeing her opportunity, Nancy jumped into the boat and grabbed Martika around the waist.

Again, the gun went off. This time, the shot hit the cave wall, sending rock splinters flying in all directions. Nancy grabbed Martika's gun hand and slammed it against the gunwale of the boat. The pistol flew into the water, where it rapidly sank to the bottom.

Martika was not through yet. Somehow she managed to push Nancy off her. Freeing her hand, Martika pulled the speedboat's throttle. The powerful little craft blasted out of the grotto so fast that Derek, bleeding from the shoulder and staggering to his feet, toppled backward, right out of the boat and into the water.

Nancy was thrown backward, too, knocking her head painfully against the gunwale. As she got to her feet, she saw George diving into the water to rescue Derek. Then, with a shudder, Nancy saw that the briefcase with the bomb was still in the boat! It was lying near the steering wheel, where Martika had dropped it during her struggle with Derek.

Before Nancy could get to it, Martika was on her and had her hands around Nancy's throat.

Nancy saw stars and knew she was on the verge of blacking out.

Summoning her last ounce of strength, Nancy reached around Martika and managed to get a hand on the steering wheel. She gave it one big yank. The responsive little speedboat nearly did a ninety-degree turn. Martika was thrown to one side, her head hitting the boat with a sharp crack. Trying to stand, she toppled into the ocean.

Nancy stared at the briefcase, which lay under the console at the front of the boat. There was no time to make a grab for it. In one motion, Nancy threw herself overboard, just as the boat exploded in a giant fireball!

Nancy disappeared under the surface just in time, and when she resurfaced, nothing was left of the boat but an oil slick and thousands of splinters of fiberglass and wood.

Swimming over to Martika, Nancy saw that the woman was sinking. This time Martika wasn't faking it.

Nancy dove, catching the unconscious Martika and positioning her so that she could carry her to shore. She only hoped Martika was alive, so that she could get what was coming to her.

Two days later Nancy and her friends were at the St. Thomas airport, waiting for the flight that would take them back to the U.S. mainland and River Heights. They were sitting at a snack bar, watching the planes taxi in and sipping glasses of cold papaya juice. George had a newspaper, which she was poring over. It was full of news about Cloud Nine.

"It says Derek's going to be released from the hospital tomorrow," George informed them. "Of course, he'll have a lot of questions to answer from the police. And get this—he's been trying to get the nurses to play cards with him! Can you believe it?" She shook her head disapprovingly.

"Once a gambler, always a gambler, I guess," Bess commented ruefully.

"I'm just glad Martika wasn't badly injured," Nancy said. Captain Logan had called the resort the day before to say that the model had been treated for a mild concussion and was in police custody now.

"I wonder how she likes the accommodations at the Charlotte Amalie jail?" George said.

"Yeah," Bess chimed in, giggling. "Do you think she's got a Jacuzzi?"

"I think Martika Sawyer's going to have to learn to live without luxuries," Nancy said. "She'll be an old lady by the time she gets out of prison—if she ever does." She gazed out the window for a minute in silence. "It still makes me furious to think of how she tried to use me. And what she did to poor Maura."

"But you didn't let her get away with it,"

George said, patting Nancy on the back. "In the end, she was no match for you."

"What does the paper say about Kurt?" Bess asked.

"Lots," George said, a smile coming over her face. "But most of it's exaggeration. For instance, it says he's been offered a three-picture deal with a big movie studio, but I happen to know it's only two."

"How do you know?" Bess prodded.

"I ran into him in the weight room at the workout center this morning while you were still packing," George explained.

"I'm sure it was just a chance meeting," Nancy teased.

George blushed and changed the subject. "You know, one of the movies he's going to do is about what happened at Cloud Nine. It's going to be called *Trouble in Paradise*. Do you think we'll be in it?"

"How could we not be?" Bess asked. "Maybe they'll even offer us parts."

Nancy laughed.

"In the meantime Kurt's going to stay on at the resort and manage things for Preston Winchell," George went on.

"I heard this morning that Cloud Nine is booked solid for the next two months. I guess a little publicity goes a long way," said Nancy. "It

149

must have really made Christina Adams mad when she found out that Winchell decided to keep Cloud Nine open."

"I loved the way she took off in her yacht yesterday," Bess added. "She sure didn't have any trouble getting it started, either."

Just then Nancy heard the boarding announcement for their flight.

"Come on, guys," she said, picking up her carry-on bag. "It's time to head out to the gate."

They were walking down the corridor when Bess suddenly stopped.

"I forgot to tell you," she said urgently. "You'll never believe it."

"What?" George asked.

"I weighed myself this morning," she said, "and I lost four pounds! I don't even know how they melted off."

Nancy and George, who'd been expecting something earth-shattering, both broke out in gales of laughter.

"I do," George said at last. "It's solving mysteries with Nancy. That'll take the extra pounds off every time."

Nancy's next case:

Nancy has come to Emerson College to spend Sweetheart Week with Ned—a Valentine's Day tradition. But this year's festivities take an ugly turn when Rosie Lopez is crowned campus Sweetheart. Her prize: a nasty knock on the head, a ride to the hospital, and an anonymous note threatening darker days and deeds to come.

The note is signed Cupid, and Nancy knows that this archer's arrows are tipped with venomous intent. The object of the stalker's wrath is Theta Pi, the sorority house where Nancy is staying. Pledging to unmask the Valentine's Day avenger, Nancy discovers that Cupid has taken aim at a new target. Suddenly she's in the line of fire . . . and terror . . . in *My Deadly Valentine,* Case #92 in The Nancy Drew Files™.

THE HARDY BOYS® CASE FILES